Brass Keys to Murder

A full list of L. Ron Hubbard's
novellas and short stories is provided at the back.

*Dekalogy—a group of ten volumes

L. RON HUBBARD

Brass Keys to Murder

GALAXY
PRESS

Published by
Galaxy Press, LLC
7051 Hollywood Boulevard, Suite 200
Hollywood, CA 90028

Printed in the United States of America.

ISBN-10 1-59212-259-0
ISBN-13 978-1-59212-259-2

Library of Congress Control Number: 2007903609

Contents

Stories from Pulp Fiction's Golden Age

A ND it *was* a golden age.
The 1930s and 1940s were a vibrant, seminal time for a gigantic audience of eager readers, probably the largest per capita audience of readers in American history. The magazine racks were chock-full of publications with ragged trims, garish cover art, cheap brown pulp paper, low cover prices—and the most excitement you could hold in your hands.

"Pulp" magazines, named for their rough-cut, pulpwood paper, were a vehicle for more amazing tales than Scheherazade could have told in a million and one nights. Set apart from higher-class "slick" magazines, printed on fancy glossy paper with quality artwork and superior production values, the pulps were for the "rest of us," adventure story after adventure story for people who liked to *read*. Pulp fiction authors were no-holds-barred entertainers—real storytellers. They were more interested in a thrilling plot twist, a horrific villain or a white-knuckle adventure than they were in lavish prose or convoluted metaphors.

The sheer volume of tales released during this wondrous golden age remains unmatched in any other period of literary history—hundreds of thousands of published stories in over nine hundred different magazines. Some titles lasted only an issue or two; many magazines succumbed to paper shortages during World War II, while others endured for decades yet. Pulp fiction remains as a treasure trove of stories you can read, stories you can love, stories you can remember. The stories were driven by plot and character, with grand heroes, terrible villains, beautiful damsels (often in distress), diabolical plots, amazing places, breathless romances. The readers wanted to be taken beyond the mundane, to live adventures far removed from their ordinary lives—and the pulps rarely failed to deliver.

In that regard, pulp fiction stands in the tradition of all memorable literature. For as history has shown, good stories are much more than fancy prose. William Shakespeare, Charles Dickens, Jules Verne, Alexandre Dumas—many of the greatest literary figures wrote their fiction for the readers, not simply literary colleagues and academic admirers. And writers for pulp magazines were no exception. These publications reached an audience that dwarfed the circulations of today's short story magazines. Issues of the pulps were scooped up and read by over thirty million avid readers each month.

Because pulp fiction writers were often paid no more than a cent a word, they had to become prolific or starve. They also had to write aggressively. As Richard Kyle, publisher and editor of *Argosy*, the first and most long-lived of the pulps, so pointedly explained: "The pulp magazine writers, the best of them, worked for markets that did not write for critics or attempt to satisfy timid advertisers. Not having to answer to anyone other than their readers, they wrote about human beings on the edges of the unknown, in those new lands the future would explore. They wrote for what we would become, not for what we had already been."

Some of the more lasting names that graced the pulps include H. P. Lovecraft, Edgar Rice Burroughs, Robert E. Howard, Max Brand, Louis L'Amour, Elmore Leonard, Dashiell Hammett, Raymond Chandler, Erle Stanley Gardner, John D. MacDonald, Ray Bradbury, Isaac Asimov, Robert Heinlein—and, of course, L. Ron Hubbard.

In a word, he was among the most prolific and popular writers of the era. He was also the most enduring—hence this series—and certainly among the most legendary. It all began only months after he first tried his hand at fiction, with L. Ron Hubbard tales appearing in *Thrilling Adventures, Argosy, Five-Novels Monthly, Detective Fiction Weekly, Top-Notch, Texas Ranger, War Birds, Western Stories,* even *Romantic Range.* He could write on any subject, in any genre, from jungle explorers to deep-sea divers, from G-men and gangsters, cowboys and flying aces to mountain climbers, hard-boiled detectives and spies. But he really began to shine when he turned his talent to science fiction and fantasy of which he authored nearly fifty novels or novelettes to forever change the shape of those genres.

Following in the tradition of such famed authors as Herman Melville, Mark Twain, Jack London and Ernest Hemingway, Ron Hubbard actually lived adventures that his own characters would have admired—as an ethnologist among primitive tribes, as prospector and engineer in hostile climes, as a captain of vessels on four oceans. He even wrote a series of articles for *Argosy,* called "Hell Job," in which he lived and told of the most dangerous professions a man could put his hand to.

Finally, and just for good measure, he was also an accomplished photographer, artist, filmmaker, musician and educator. But he was first and foremost a *writer,* and that's the L. Ron Hubbard we come to know through the pages of this volume.

This library of Stories from the Golden Age presents the best of L. Ron Hubbard's fiction from the heyday of storytelling, the Golden Age of the pulp magazines. In these eighty volumes, readers are treated to a full banquet of 153 stories, a kaleidoscope of tales representing every imaginable genre: science fiction, fantasy, western, mystery, thriller, horror, even romance—action of all kinds and in all places.

Because the pulps themselves were printed on such inexpensive paper with high acid content, issues were not meant to endure. As the years go by, the original issues of every pulp from *Argosy* through *Zeppelin Stories* continue crumbling into brittle, brown dust. This library preserves the L. Ron Hubbard tales from that era, presented with a distinctive look that brings back the nostalgic flavor of those times.

L. Ron Hubbard's Stories from the Golden Age has something for every taste, every reader. These tales will return you to a time when fiction was good clean entertainment and the most fun a kid could have on a rainy afternoon or the best thing an adult could enjoy after a long day at work.

Pick up a volume, and remember what reading is supposed to be all about. Remember curling up with a *great story.*

—Kevin J. Anderson

KEVIN J. ANDERSON *is the author of more than ninety critically acclaimed works of speculative fiction, including The Saga of Seven Suns, the continuation of the Dune Chronicles with Brian Herbert, and his* New York Times *bestselling novelization of L. Ron Hubbard's* Ai! Pedrito!

Brass Keys to Murder

CHAPTER ONE

The Law Comes for Stephen Craig

LIEUTENANT Stephen Craig, attired in white duty belt and blue serge uniform, leaned against the rail of the USS *Burnham* and watched the shore boat come out toward him through the fog. The muffled stutter of its exhaust grew clearer.

Steve Craig, at present officer of the deck, was interested in the shore boat only because it alone was moving in this quiet harbor. The bluish landing light fell upon his features, showing them to be big and rugged. His jaw was as square as a clipper's mainsail and his eyes were the shade of an arctic sea. His white-topped cap was set over one ear, and its golden spread eagle was tarnished by the impacts of many seas and the dampness of countless fogs—fogs of the Thames, the Huangpu, Colón.

He was obviously a destroyer man, bearing the stamp of lurching, giddy decks, smashing waves and full speed ahead.

The shore boat, a chunky affair, rapped against the landing stage, bobbing in the gentle, greasy swell. A man dressed in dirty dungarees held the lines and tried to aid the person who stepped out.

Steve Craig's brows lifted in surprise. A girl had bridged the gap and her high-heeled slippers were pounding up the spotless ladder toward the deck. She glanced up, displaying a small, well-set face presided over by a pair of great dark eyes which were deep and liquid and troubled.

"Sally!" Steve cried. "What's the idea of coming out here this time of night?"

She clattered on up and the shore boat swung away, heading back to the docks. Sally's small hand fastened on a stanchion.

"I know you've got the duty, Steve, and that I shouldn't be here, but . . . but this is serious. You've got to get away from here. I've brought some money and you can run before they come."

"Run! Before who comes? Quiet down, child, and tell me—"

"Steve, your father died tonight. He . . . he was murdered!"

"Murdered! My father? But . . . why, I've got to get ashore right away! I can get somebody to relieve me. I'll call for a boat and we'll—"

"No, Steve. They're coming up here—the police, I mean. And they . . . they're going to arrest you for the murder!"

"*Me!*" Steve's eyes widened with amazement. "But why should I want to kill Dad?"

"They know that you and your father didn't get along, Steve, and that—"

"But, Sally! We patched that all up weeks ago, just before he sailed for Panama on his last trip. He was coming out here tonight to see me. Just got in this afternoon, and I've had the watch all day—all afternoon, I mean."

"Have you any letters from him or anything like that to show that you patched everything up?"

4

"No . . . he never wrote to anybody. Sally, they can't pin this thing on me. Why, I've been right here on this deck since noon!"

"But who's been with you since five o'clock?"

"Nobody much. Billy Reynolds came up and talked for a while and then went ashore. Most of the crew is on liberty, and it's been too foggy to stay up on deck tonight for movies. The quartermaster isn't feeling so good, and I let him go down to the sick bay an hour or so ago."

"Can't you get someone to say . . . look, Steve! Here comes the police launch! You haven't time to do anything. They'll make you—"

The harbor patrol boat, its stern crowded with men, shoved out of the black mist and banged hard against the landing stage, making the platform creak. Men began to get out. Each time one reached the stage, he looked up at the deck, cautiously, before he clambered up the ladder. There were four in all. Haggarty, Detective-Sergeant Green and two officers. The boat swung away to circle and wait.

Green stepped down to the curving steel deck and looked around, mouthing a cigar. His overcoat collar was turned up and his small eyes were set far back in the folds of his face.

"Hello, Craig," he said. "I'm afraid you'll have to come along with us. There's a little matter—oh, beg pardon, Miss Randolph," he said, tipping his hard hat. "I see you got here with the news before we did. Know all about it, do you, Craig? How we found the body, I mean."

"... look, Steve! Here comes the police launch!
You haven't time to do anything."

"I only know that my father is dead."

"Of course I expected you to claim ignorance of the works—they always do. You'd better come along with us right now. We'll put you in out of this fog where you won't catch cold."

"You can belay the wisecracks, Green. Let's hear some more about this affair."

Green looked at Steve's arctic eyes and shrugged. "All right. But you're just wasting time, that's all. We found Jeremiah Craig's body about an hour and a half ago, floating near the docks. He got it with a knife in his side. German clasp knife. We pulled him out, and I got busy. I used to have this beat about ten years ago, before they made a sergeant out of me and put me in the homicide squad. And I know all about the fuss you kicked up by running away to the Naval Academy instead of going to a merchant marine school. And you knew all the time how much old Craig hated the Navy."

"You can skip that," said Steve. "How do you figure I killed him? I've been officer of the deck since noon, because we're short of officers. And you know that I haven't left this ship. Look at the log over there if you don't believe me."

Green stepped to the tilted desk and glanced at the huge book which lay open upon it. Coming back to Craig, he worked his cigar over into the corner of his mouth.

"That hasn't anything to do with it," he said. "When old Craig docked this afternoon he heard you were in port. And he decided it was about time he came over and gave you a lacing. And so when you were alone on deck he came up the gangplank swearing at you. And you grabbed out your knife

7

and shoved it into his ribs. It was foggy and it was dark and nobody saw it at all."

"Go on," said Steve grimly.

"I figure it that way because the body was found south from this boat. And the tide was ebbing in that direction three or four hours ago."

"Green," said Steve, "you ought to have been a sailor. As a cop, you're a dud."

"Look here, young fellow—"

"While I'm standing on this deck you'll address me as lieutenant. As to your dumbness—"

Sally Randolph stepped between them. "Don't fight, please."

Steve pushed her gently to one side, without looking at her. "As to your dumbness, Jeremiah Craig and I made up that old quarrel weeks ago. And he wanted to see me this trip to have dinner with me. I saw him on his last cruise."

"Were there any witnesses to that?" barked Green.

"No. We met on the dock late one night."

"Why didn't you knife him that time? Wasn't your alibi good enough?"

"Keep a civil tongue in your head, Green," Steve snapped. "You may think you can come aboard this ship with two armed policemen and a fathead detective and tell me where to head in, but you're half-seas over, get me?" He patted his duty belt and the holstered .45 which dangled from the webbing. The two policemen stepped back, glancing hurriedly down the gangway to make certain that it was clear.

Green laughed. "Making a show, aren't you? I talked with your brother Jim tonight before I came up here. He's in on an

Insular boat. And he didn't know anything about this patched up business."

"Jim's been around the Horn," said Steve. "I haven't seen him for six months."

"And," smiled Green, "I talked with old Andries up on Ship Street, and *he* didn't know anything about it."

"I haven't seen Andries this cruise."

"Maybe not. But he's seen you ashore. Tells me he's been trying to get in touch with you. Old friend of your father's, isn't he?"

"Yes. Mate with him on the *Mary Anne* in the China Sea in 1912. Why bring him into it?"

"And I saw Hawkins—Brant Hawkins." Green took out his cigar, admired its tattered length and replaced it. "He's after your hide. After all, your dad used to captain for Hawkins."

"Maybe he did," snapped Steve. "But Hawkins and Dad have been on the outs for the last year and a half. Why do you think Dad went over to the Insular Line and left Hawkins' ships?"

"I'm not worrying about that," said Green. "You better come along, young fellow. We'll give you a fair enough trial."

"I suppose you would," replied Steve, his gaze level—"and then hang me at the end of it!"

"Naw," said Haggarty. "We'd hang you at the end of a rope."

Steve's raking eyes stopped the laugh before it had begun.

"Come along," said Green. "I've had enough of this."

"I'm not going anywhere," rapped Steve. "And I'll thank you to get off this ship immediately."

"Take the gun away from him, boys!" Green ordered.

"You mean you're demanding my sidearms?"

"Sure. Why not?"

"Because I cannot surrender my sidearms to anyone but a superior officer. Green, I'll remind you that you're standing on the deck of a warship of the United States Navy."

"What does that make me?"

Steve's set jaw jutted out. "I do not happen to be liable to civil arrest so long as I stand on this deck. If you want to take me, you'll have to see the Judge Advocate General down in Washington, and he'll have to investigate this matter before anything can be done about it."

"Yeah?" said Green.

"Yes. And I'll give you three to get into that canoe of yours and beat it!"

Green made a motion to the police. The two bluecoats stepped forward, gingerly, hands wrapped tight about their nightsticks.

Steve did not seem to move, but the first officer rocketed through the air and slammed into a steel bulkhead. The second lurched into the rail, hung perilously for a moment and then crashed through, taking a stanchion with him. The dull splash of his body came up to them through the fog, followed immediately by his frantic cries to the patrol boat.

The launch swept in, boathook ready, bent on rescue work. Haggarty backed up, spun about, and ran down the ladder. Green glared at Steve who shrugged his coat into position across his broad shoulders.

"This boat sails in three days," snarled Green. "It would take your Judge Advocate General that long to make up his mind about this case. We'll have you off here in forty-eight hours, and we'll have your shiny little stripes. And after that we'll have the pleasure of hanging you for murder."

Green walked down the ladder to the waiting boat. The drenched policeman sat shivering in the amidship section.

From the stern of the launch, Green looked up and shook his fist. "And don't you try to get ashore either. Navy or no Navy, if you set foot on land we can arrest you in two seconds and make it stick!"

"Can they?" said Sally in a small voice.

Steve watched the launch speed away and then turned his attention to a bruised set of knuckles.

"Sure they can," he said. "But that isn't going to stop me from settling this case on my own."

CHAPTER TWO

Steve Takes His Chance Ashore

WHEN the staccato clangs of eight bells had died away, denoting the hour of midnight, Ensign Billy Reynolds came on deck to relieve Steve. "Why so morose?" he demanded. "You look too glum for a bridegroom-to-be. What's the matter—Sally throw you over?"

"No. They're trying to hang a murder on me, Billy. My father was killed early this evening."

"I'm sorry. I . . . I . . ."

"That's all right."

"It takes a while for something like this to sink in!"

"I know it does. I'm all in a fog myself."

Ensign Reynolds leaned against the rail, frowning. "That's tough. And we had everything set for the wedding. Had some nice presents for you and Sally, too. Guess that's all off now, isn't it?"

"No, I hope not. Sally's going to help me out all she can. I told the skipper awhile ago and he offered to let me use the boats or anything I wanted, but I wouldn't take them."

"Why not?"

"Don't want to get the skipper in trouble. Things are bad enough as they are. They'll arrest me if I'm spotted ashore, but all I can do is go ashore and try to straighten this thing out before the JAG gets hold of it and turns me over to them."

"It ought not take them more than forty-eight hours to get the JAG's ear," said Reynolds. "And that doesn't work out. If we sailed before they could get the orders out, you'd have a chance to stay with us. As it is, you'll be ashore a day before we sail."

"I'm going to do what I can," said Steve. "Sally is bringing a skiff out here—should be here now. We'll land at some old pier and go up to see a fellow by the name of Andries. He should know all about my father's business. If I can find the real reason Dad was killed, I can spot the criminal and everything will be jake. I told her to have some other people there, too."

Reynolds nodded. "Well, I've got the deck and you're as free as a sea gull. And I didn't even see you leave."

Steve walked aft toward the fantail. The curling wisps of fog wove in and out of the depth charge rack and wrapped damp folds about the naked flagstaff. Leaning over the fantail edge, Steve spotted the rowboat which bobbed in the gray shadows below.

"Sally!" he hissed.

"All set, Steve. Slide down."

He laid hold of a line and lowered himself into the thwarts. A black boatman looked at him stolidly from between the oarlocks and then shoved off.

The rhythmic dipping of the oars was almost soundless. Ships floated by as though painted on a dim, blurred screen. Sally Randolph, wrapped in a glistening, thin slicker, sat silent beside Steve, looking up at him from time to time as though to make certain that he was still there.

The boatman guided the stubby craft in toward an age-slimed landing stage at the foot of Ship Street. He shipped his oars, secured the painter and looked up.

"Wait until we come back," said Sally.

But Steve shook his head and reached into his pocket pulling forth a dollar bill. "We might not come back," he said meaningly.

"Ah'll wait," said the boatman, putting the money into a decrepit wallet. "Nothin' to do nohow."

Sally and Steve went up the stage to the dock. Steve examined the dim street before them, watching for any sign of a policeman.

"I feel as though I'd really done something," he said. "But if they hauled me in, we'd have to depend upon that dumb flatfoot Green to ferret this case, and I'd miss my ship. And that, Miss Sally, would be the end of a future admiral."

They made their way between silent, dark buildings, which smelled of pine tar and oakum, until they found the number ten on the front of a house. Steve went up the steps and knocked.

In a moment they heard a chair scrape on the other side of the door. Then a face appeared at a side window. Presently the sound of heavy bolts creaked through the dampness and Andries bowed them in.

Andries was still shy of sixty, but he looked much older. His too-bright small eyes regarded them beadily. His gray hair was sparse and tangled. He walked before them, limping, favoring his artificial leg. He had lost the real limb, it was said, in the China Sea, and the occurrence had been the turning point of his life. But no one would deny that Andries—Joel Andries—knew his ships, nor that he knew all the doings along the waterfront.

"In the next room," said Andries in a creaking voice, "I've got your brother and Hawkins and a young German by the name of Kloss. They're all I could find that knew your dad real well. And they're the only ones that had much to do with him in this port."

"Thanks, Andries."

"Don't thank me, young bucko. I'm owing a right lot more than that to your dad. And I'm just as set as you are on bringing the murderer to justice. It's a privilege to be of help—especially to such a pretty young lady as Miss Randolph." He smiled. "Before we go in and talk to these people, maybe you've got something you'd like to say to me, privatelike."

"I would like to ask you what your opinion is," said Steve.

"That's the worst of it." Andries' bushy brows met in a frown. "I haven't got the smallest kind of an idea about where to begin. Any man that was crook enough to kill your dad deserves to be brought up and hung. And if they don't do it—the police—I'll do it myself, with my bare hands." Andries nodded vigorously. "I sailed too many years with your dad, Steve."

"Let's go in," said Sally.

The inner room was a drab affair. Ship models were placed about the walls, but their bright paint was dulled by dust, and the odor of strong sailor's tobacco was rank in the room. The only shining objects were those constructed of brass, and these were brightly polished—two cuspidors, a set of chest corners and a naked cutlass.

On the far side of the room, Brant Hawkins struggled to his feet. He wore a wing collar, a precisely pressed coat and he carried a carved cane which he held, with his hat and gloves, in his left hand.

"Hello, Craig," said Hawkins smoothly. "I hear you're in trouble."

"So do I," replied Steve.

Jim Craig, mate's cap on the back of his head, stood up with a hard grin and nodded to Sally. "They caught up with the black sheep at last," he commented. He looked like Steve in a way, but he bore the stamp of a loser, different school.

Kloss, the German sailor, shifted uneasy feet and fumbled with a felt hat.

"Let's get down to business," said Steve. "I want to know all that you folks know about Jeremiah Craig's affairs these last few years."

"We don't know very much, I'm afraid," said Hawkins. "We've been talking here, waiting until you came, and we haven't reached any conclusion whatever."

"Except," corrected Andries, "that somebody had it in for Jeremiah Craig bad enough to kill him."

"Well, er, yes," replied Hawkins. "Since he left my employ—"

"Why did he leave your employ?" asked Steve.

"Well, er, you see, he and I had a . . . well, an argument over a cargo. Jeremiah declared that he wouldn't go down to . . . to Peru after a cargo of . . ." He hesitated, turning a dull red. "He wouldn't go down after this cargo because he said it was beneath his dignity to carry such stuff. And I told him . . . well, I told him that I could find plenty of captains who would and he . . . well, he quit."

"And since that time," said Steve, "you've sold out to the Insular people."

"You bet he has!" creaked Andries. "Since Jeremiah was with them, the Insular people got plenty of cargoes they never even dreamed about getting. And I heard that *you* and Craig had an argument last year over that same thing, Hawkins."

Hawkins jerked his head at Andries. "What if I did?" he rapped. "Craig always was a hotheaded old—"

"What was that again?" said Jim Craig.

"I beg your pardon."

Steve turned to Kloss. "Where do you come in?"

"I don't know. He—that old guy over there—he picked me up in a flophouse and made me come up here."

Andries bristled. "Old guy, is it? I ought to take you apart—and I would too, if it wasn't for my game leg! You were fired off Jeremiah's ship last cruise. He kicked you down the gangway and told you never to come back."

"And I know it," said Jim Craig, readjusting his cap. "The old man never told me all of it, but it was a pretty mess to hear him sputter. You were trying to bring a cargo of your own through, weren't you, Kloss?"

"I don't know anything about it," said Kloss sullenly, his eyes on the floor. He moved his thick legs and fumbled again with his hat, twisting the brim.

Jim Craig stood up. "Maybe if I beat a little sense—"

"Wait a minute, Jim!" admonished Steve. "We've had enough bloodshed to last quite a while."

Kloss stared dumbly at Jim Craig. "You ain't going to make me talk any." He shifted his steadfast gaze to Hawkins and kept it there.

"We'll deal with you later," said Steve. "Now listen, Andries, I remember hearing of some doings on the last cruise of the *Mary Anne*. You were aboard her, weren't you?"

"Sure. I was mate of her, wasn't I?"

"And I was the midshipman," volunteered Jim.

"You were a damned ordinary seaman," Andries corrected. "And we carried you on the books like that, though you never drew pay. And you were eight years old."

"Maybe," admitted Jim. "But I was there, wasn't I? And when those pirates climbed us in the Yellow Sea—"

"China Sea!" snapped Andries. "You don't know anything about it!"

"I know a lot more than you think." Jim's grin was hard.

"What happened on that cruise?" insisted Steve.

"It was like this," Andries said. "Some of the boys got a little persnickety and tried to mob the rest of us. Bad food, poor pay, long time between ports—you know the story."

"Do you suppose any of those men are alive today?"

"I doubt it. That was in 1912, and a man don't carry a grudge that long. I've even forgotten what those boys' names were."

"I haven't," said Jim. "There was—"

"Let it pass," said Steve. "Andries is right. Too long ago. But we haven't gotten anywhere at all. These aren't any reasons

19

to kill a man—an argument over a cargo, a fired seaman, a mutinous crew."

Sally leaned forward in her chair. "But any of those reasons might go a lot deeper than you think, Steve."

Hawkins coughed. "If you don't mind, it's rather late. I think I had better be getting home."

"Me too," said Kloss, jumping up, his face suddenly eager.

"I'm going to go to work on these things tonight," said Steve. "Where was Dad's boat wharfed?"

"Down at Dock Eighteen. They found his body floating near there, too." Andries stroked his chin. "You aren't going down there, are you, Steve?"

"Sure. I want to look through his papers before these dumb police get wise to the fact that papers might exist. And I'll have to work fast."

"Okay," said Jim Craig. "It's your own neck, Stevie." He stood up. "Want me to help you?"

Steve shook his head.

"Better not, Jim. You'll endanger your own reputation. Any kind of scandal in the merchant service is bad stuff."

"How about the naval service?" said Jim, grinning.

"I'll get this settled one way or another," Steve replied. "I only wish to God I could find out what anybody had against Dad that would make them want to kill him! And I'd dig right ahead and find out even if I didn't have the finger on my neck. You'd better scout around some, too, Jim. And do some remembering. I'll get in touch with you."

Hawkins sidled toward the door and bowed his way out.

Kloss followed him without any bow. Jim went down the passage humming thoughtfully.

Andries shook Steve's hand. "Any help I can give, Steve, just let me know."

"Thanks, Andries. I'll give you a tip."

Andries looked up, his eyes sharp.

"What's that?"

Steve smiled grimly. "The murderer of Jeremiah Craig was in this room tonight!"

CHAPTER THREE

Sergeant Green Means Trouble

PIER Eighteen's warehouse was nothing more than a collection of fog-grayed shadows steeped in dismal silence, unrelieved by lights. The SS *Mandarin*, Jeremiah Craig's weather-scarred freighter, queen of the Insular Line, was motionless and dark beside the wharf, its bulk showing only one light—the gangway lantern.

The after-midnight silence had settled on the waterfront—the thick, heavy silence of stupor rather than sleep. The *Mandarin* should have been engaged in unloading, but with its captain gone, the cargo booms spraddled stiffly out; its black winches, dotted by globes of moisture, were silent. It would be morning—and late morning, at that—before the crew and owners recovered from the shock of losing Jeremiah Craig.

Sally Randolph and Steve approached the dock with slow, cautious steps. Sally's raincoat and small hat glistened with drops of water. Steve's uniform was damp, its gold braid, tarnished by many seas, was dull with moisture.

"I'd better scout around," whispered Steve. "There might be a watchman."

"And there might be police," agreed Sally. "Do you want me to wait out here?"

"No. Go back and find that boatman and have him bring

the skiff under the *Mandarin*'s stern. I'll give you a five-minute start."

Sally nodded and walked away, glancing back apprehensively at the ominously quiet ship. Steve watched her, sorrow in his eyes. By rights Sally Randolph should be home—uptown in that great stone house—sleeping peacefully in expectation of a heavy day's work on the morrow: The work of packing and assembling her clothes, of telling excited friends all about it—how she would follow Steve on a passenger ship down to Guantánamo for the winter maneuvers. Steve wondered if she had told her folks about the murder yet. He hoped not. He didn't want anyone worried on his account or on Sally's.

When Steve's wristwatch stated that five minutes had elapsed, he moved from shadow to shadow down the outside of the warehouse, toward the gangway. He hoped the watch would be elsewhere, or not anywhere at all. Still, on Jeremiah Craig's ships, a watch was always kept, in port and at sea.

When he had breasted the towering whitish bulk of the superstructure, he scrutinized the decks. He would have to pass the top of the gangway, walk the breadth of the ship and mount two ladders to the bridge and Jeremiah Craig's quarters. And somewhere along that devious route he stood too good a chance of accosting a sailor or officer. Certainly they did not know him, but he looked like Jeremiah Craig and they would be able to guess. Of course they knew about the murder by this time. True, it hadn't reached the papers; Green was not so big a fool as that.

Throwing back his shoulders, Steve went up the gangway, his feet soundless on the slippery cleats. The smell of paint and coal smoke and old cargoes assailed his nostrils—the incense of the merchant sailor.

Almost to the top, the glare of the gangway light struck him full in the face. Beyond the light he saw something glitter and ducked his head, and hurriedly moved out of the light.

An impersonal voice accosted him from the shadows. "What's your business, mister?"

Steve made out the glint of a police badge and the shimmer of brass buttons. A nightstick swung by its cord from the policeman's wrist. Steve could not see the face. He decided to bluff it out.

"Chief Officer Hardesty reporting aboard." There was an annoyed growl in his voice.

The officer stepped forward and looked under Steve's cap brim. "What business?"

"What business have you got aboard an Insular boat?" snapped Steve.

"The captain of this ship was killed. We're watching it, that's all."

Steve breathed a sigh of relief. The officer had probably mistaken the naval uniform for that of the Insular line—a common enough mistake with landlubbers.

Steve grunted and walked by as though going to his quarters. The policeman watched him from the top of the gangway. Steve turned into a passageway, walked the length of it, turned and walked down another. Opening a door, he stepped over the high sill and mounted the ladders to the bridge.

All was silence there. A white sign with blue letters, "Captain," was posted over a door. Steve tried the latch and found that the door was open. He went in quickly. His hands fumbled for the shutters and curtains at the window, found them and drew them. He was about to throw the light switch when a hunch seized hold of him.

Stepping catlike to the deck, he made his way to the inboard rail and looked down at the gangway. It was unguarded. A sound of hurrying steps came from the upper end of the pier.

Steve swore to himself. The officer had had his suspicions, after all. He was headed for a phone and reserves. And he would find out that no such man as Hardesty was in the employ of the Insular Line. Steve wished despairingly that he had known a real chief officer's name to give the cop.

Moving quickly, he went back to the cabin, battened the door and turned on the light. The light oak woodwork was spotless and shining. The brass handrails of the locker glowed brightly. Along the wall were pictures of ships and more ships. Wooden ships and steel ships. These had been the commands of Jeremiah Craig, and each and every vessel had escaped the ravages of the sea under his competent hands.

Above the desk, framed in leather, were two pictures. One was from the *Log of Annapolis*. The other was clipped from a newspaper. And they were both of Steve! He stared blankly at them. Something like a wad of dry cotton waste clogged his throat. He turned and looked at the top of the locker. Another photo was there. One of Steve dressed as a midshipman. This, too, had been clipped from a newspaper, probably appearing over the heading of some account of athletic honors. But there was something wrong with this picture. It had been marked with pencil. On closer examination Steve found that the insignia of the merchant marine had been superimposed over the insignia of the navy on both collar and cap.

How many thousands of sea leagues had Jeremiah Craig traveled alone in this cabin with those tattered, poorly reproduced pictures?

Steve, with an effort, jerked himself out of his reverie. He turned to the neat desk where cargo manifests were stacked. Pulling open the drawers, he plunged a hurried hand through the contents. But these were all papers dealing with Insular Line business. Steve stood back in the center of the room, looking about him, frowning. His eye fell on a carved camphor wood chest, secured by a brass lock of mammoth proportions. Kneeling, he tried to unfasten the hasp, but it was unrelenting. He stopped for a moment, listening for the approach of footsteps. But no sound came.

Steve opened the locker. A small drawer was at the top, unlocked. He opened it and found a mass of uniform buttons. Rattling them aside, he saw the dull steel of a key at the bottom. He went back to the chest and applied the key. The hasp came open.

Throwing back the lid, Steve saw a tray filled with white cap covers and white jackets, laid away for the next tropical cruise. He lifted it out and his eyes fell on neatly folded blue uniforms. Frowning, he started to replace the tray, then stopped. Footsteps were tapping the old timbers of the dock down below.

The tray would not fit immediately. Steve tugged at it. Suddenly he saw that it had a false bottom. No wonder the thing was so heavy! A catch on the end allowed the tray to part along a cleverly hidden line. The Chinese workmanship was perfect.

Tattered, sea-beaten logs, tied bundles of letters, brown envelopes crammed with age-browned receipts. Steve pulled a suitcase out of the locker and crammed it full, strapping it. The thing was heavy, unwieldy, but he could do no better.

He was about to shut off the lights when his glance fell on the waste basket—a woven affair from Haiti. Only one envelope was there. Not knowing why he did so, Steve pulled it out and thrust it into his pocket.

Footsteps were coming up the gangway. Retreat was cut off in that direction. Steve looked down. Police caps bobbed beneath his eyes. He looked along the boat deck, spotted a ladder at the far end and ran aft, the suitcase banging against his legs.

He slid down the ladder, found another and descended it, stopped, and found that he was on the after well deck. He made his way over tarpaulins and lines to the outboard rail and looked down. He whistled softly, but there was no response.

Crossing the deck, he called from the other side. Still no answer. A small light was burning at the dock end, and by its glow he could see no sign of the skiff, the boatman or Sally.

Voices, gruff, excited, whipped down from the bridge. A whining voice, belonging, probably, to a steward aroused from sleep, came clearly to Steve.

"Naw!" it said. "There ain't any chief officer named Hardesty in the whole Insular outfit. What's the matter with you guys?"

And another voice snarled, "Never mind what's the matter with us. Steve Craig came aboard this ship a few minutes ago, get me? Steve Craig, the man who killed your captain. This dumb flatfoot was too scared to tackle him. Turn out the crew. We'll search this tub from stem to stern. He won't get away!"

Steve swallowed hard. That second voice belonged to Green. Wildly, Steve looked for the skiff. If he were caught now, he wouldn't have a ghost of a chance. They'd throw him into the jail and let him stay there for months, before they even so much as gave him a preliminary hearing. And with Green on the job, after today Steve wouldn't have a rowboat's show in a howling typhoon.

Some of the ship's officers were coming out on deck. Lights were clicked on in the fog. Steve looked up at the powerful loading lights, which hung halfway up the mast above him. If they shot those on, the deck where he stood would be turned into day.

He looked about him and laid hands on a length of halyard line which was coiled about the ratlines. Bending this around the handle of the suitcase, he secured it with a bowline. Hand over hand he eased the suitcase down toward the water. When it hung a foot above the greasy surface, he secured the other end about a belaying pin.

Before he could turn, a glare of light crashed about him. They had swung on the loading spots, and he was standing in plain sight from the boat deck. Faces bobbed up there.

A voice shouted, "There he is! Get him!"

Steve jumped for the ladder which led up to the fantail deck. A shot lashed at him. The bullet yowled away into the fog.

He ducked behind a row of lashed barrels and crawled aft on all fours. The shouts were diminishing. Feet were clanging down the iron rungs of the ladder.

Steve took off his cap, doubled it up and shoved it into his belt. The crazy, obtuse thought that caps cost fifteen dollars raced through his mind. But before it was gone, he had knifed out through space in a swan dive. The greasy water came up, the surface parted with scarcely more than a ripple and let him down into the depths.

He turned himself about, holding air in bursting lungs, and struck out for the wharf and the protection of pilings. He came up. The stern of the *Mandarin* was high above his head. The white depth scale reared like a small ladder. The tip of the brass propeller was out, and Steve noted with an odd abstraction that they must have unloaded the after hold first.

Then he was under again, swimming steadily. When his head came out the second time, a piling was at his right. He clung to its slimy roundness, looking for the skiff, hoping that it would not be spotted from the deck of the freighter.

The creak of an oarlock came to him from some place near. His grip on the piling was insecure, and he treaded water with his legs, holding his head out. He called out in a low voice.

To his strained ears came the answer, "That you, Steve?"

"Over here. Beside this piling. Make it snappy! I'm almost drowned!"

The oarlocks creaked, as oars were shipped. The boatman was passing the skiff from piling to piling with his hands.

Steve laid hold of the gunwale. The boatman snatched at his collar and yanked him into the bottom. Little rivers of water, suddenly cold, ran down inside Steve's clothes. He pulled the cap out of his belt, whipped some of the water out of it and put it on. Streams ran down on either side of his face.

Sally helped him up on a thwart and hugged him. "I couldn't find the boatman right away, Steve. I'm so sorry, I—"

"That's all right," said Steve. "Look out, I'm getting you all wet. I left a suitcase dangling on the inboard side of the *Mandarin*. Maybe we'll be able to get it in a few minutes. Hear all that yelling?"

"They spotted you! I was so afraid they would. Was it worth the risk?"

Steve shrugged. "We'll find out tomorrow. I'm all worn-out."

At Steve's direction, the stolid boatman guided the skiff in under the rail of the *Mandarin*, where it was almost wholly protected by the dock and steep ship side.

Voices were calling from the decks above them and men were running to and fro, pulling bales apart, clambering in and out of dark corners.

"They don't know I went over the side," Steve whispered. "There's the suitcase." He reached out with an oar and brought it to them. The boatman brought out a knife and cut the line, no sign of curiosity on his seemingly frozen face.

"Shove off," said Steve. "We'll go underneath this dock and leave from the other side. The warehouse will mask our trip to the destroyer."

"I hope so!" breathed Sally.

The skiff went steadily on, changing course occasionally, where the piling did not stand in straight lines. In a few minutes they were out in the empty fog of the harbor.

The riding lights of the destroyer neared. The boatman started to make for the gangway, but Steve caught hold of an oar.

"No," said Steve, "they might have a patrol boat looking for me to come aboard that side. Go in under the fantail."

The boatman bobbed his woolly bare head and with two swift strokes sent the skiff bubbling through the water in that direction. He stood up and caught the line Steve had used in the descent earlier in the night, passing it back to Steve.

With the line in his hand, Steve made quick work of lashing it to the suitcase. Then he stood up, balancing himself. Sally looked up at him and with a swift move he stooped and kissed her.

About to ascend once more, he again turned. "I'll bet I ruined that letter I found in the waste basket."

"What letter?"

Steve drew it out. The envelope had fallen apart and water ran from the folds. He laid the paper down on a thwart and by the glow of the truck light, read its penciled printing aloud.

"'Send,'" read Steve, "'the brass keys to me. Otherwise I will kill first for vengeance, second for caution and third for profit.'"

Sally and Steve stared blankly at each other.

CHAPTER FOUR

A .38 Raps Challenge

I T was night again, night overcast with the gray shadows of fog. The sounds of the night-blanketed harbor were mellowed by the mist; among them came the creak of an oarlock, and a low whistle.

Steve Craig leaned over the fantail of the *Burnham* and stared at the skiff, making certain that it was really Sally Randolph, and not the police laying a trap for him.

Steve's face was tired. His eyes, feverishly bright, were odd against his pallor. He slid down a line and balanced himself on a thwart. The boatman looked at him stolidly. For a fleeting moment, Steve felt something mysterious behind that ebon mask. And then Sally was pulling him down to the seat and he forgot all about it.

Sally's voice trembled with subdued excitement. "Did you find out anything, Steve?"

"Several things. And when the cock crows in the morning, orders will be handed to the skipper to set me ashore in the custody of the police. We received a radiogram to that effect this afternoon."

"Tomorrow morning! Why, Steve, it's seven o'clock now. You have less than twelve hours to get at the bottom of the murder!"

"Twelve hours," Steve said, "is half of one day. And although Rome was not built in a day, it took only one night to burn it down."

"What do you mean?"

"That I'm going to burn it down, that's all. There isn't any use playing with this thing. The only thing we can do is get in there, force the killer's hand, and establish why he killed my father. This isn't any time for delicate diplomats and doffed chapeaus. It's 'Full speed ahead and damn the torpedoes!' I told you, Sally, that tomorrow would see us married. We'll be—well, married or buried. And I'm going to go south with the *Burnham* or get killed trying."

"That sounds grim, Steve."

"Maybe so. But I mean it. Now listen to me, Sally. I've got a few things to get off my chest before we hit the beach. A fellow by the name of Bleak Fanshaw has those keys. And he'll either turn them over to me or he'll wish he had. That's the first thing I'm going to do, and I'll do it up right."

"How do you know, Steve? What do the keys belong to?"

"To about a half million dollars in merchandise and fabric, as nearly as I can make out. I don't know whether or not this is the right track, but I'm barreling it with my safety valves tied down.

"Sally, I found a lot of dope in those log books today. Here's one here. It's too dark to read it, so I'll tell you about it. You take it and keep it. I might need a pair of free hands the minute we set foot on the dock."

"All right, Steve."

"Here's the dope. In that log book are two things: a letter

from Brant Hawkins, and a warehouse receipt, signed by Brant Hawkins, for one of his wharves. Sally, there's something fishy here, damned fishy. I've got a motive—of sorts—that I might be able to clinch."

"You mean it, Steve?"

"Yes. We have something to go on. Listen. When I was running through those log books I found on the *Mandarin*, I uncovered one from the 1912 voyage of the *Mary Anne*. To be short and not so sweet about it, there was a mutiny aboard that ship out in the Yellow Sea. It doesn't say much in there about it. It came after an attack of pirates—Chinese pirates, evidently out of the Gulf of Chihli.

"These pirates were a pretty tough lot—still are. They used to tackle anything they sighted. It seems they sighted the steamer *Mary Anne* off the coast and set after her in their big seagoing junks—heavily armed ships with carronades and all that. They tackled the steamer, boarded her, killed several of the crew. The crew fought back as best they could with sailors' knives and a couple of rifles that were aboard.

"Midway through the fight, Jeremiah Craig picked up a rocket, ignited it and ripped it into the midst of the pirates. The rocket was red. Dad followed it up with a blue, and then a yellow. The effect on the pirates was terrific. They hadn't seen the source of the rockets, and they thought their gods were firing on them with lightning, so they tried to retreat. My father cut them down with a rifle.

"That was the finish of the pirates. Their junks were heavily loaded, and before he gave the order to scuttle them, Dad inspected their cargoes. It seems that these junks had not had time to unload since their last raids and the holds were filled with giant chests full of silk and ornaments and necklaces—anything of great value they had found on hapless, helpless ships. And so Dad gave the orders to transfer the stuff over to the *Mary Anne*."

"But I wouldn't think that that would make enemies, Steve."

"You don't know men, Sally. The situation became acute. The sailors wanted a bigger share than they thought they would get, and my father wouldn't divide until he had consulted Hawkins, the owner of the *Mary Anne*."

"Then Brant Hawkins owned Captain Craig's ship!"

"Right. So the crew, dissatisfied, mutinied. Right about there in the log, the writing is all blurred. I couldn't get the full details. But it must have been a serious fight. Andries was the first mate of the *Mary Anne*, you know, and he was reported later in the log to be doing better after a leg amputation."

"So that's how he lost his leg!"

"That's the way," said Steve. "Now I'm not sure about all this. I've got to have some outside evidence. And the only way I can get it is through Bleak Fanshaw."

"Who is he?"

"The owner of the flophouse called the 'Binnacle.' He seems to have kept some of Dad's accounts, judging from the records. If he hasn't got the keys, then I'll make him tell who has got them."

"You're clever, Steve. When you wanted to board the *Mandarin* I was worried."

"Well, I got the books anyway. Oh, yes—there's that letter from Hawkins, too. Hawkins wrote Dad that the 'goods' were not to be shared equally between members of the crew. He said that Dad did not happen to be sailing under letters of mark and reprisal—that the *Mary Anne* was not a privateersman. It looks as if Hawkins was worried about his share of the booty."

"That looks bad for Hawkins, doesn't it?"

Steve nodded.

He watched the approach of the landing stage. The boatman eased up, letting the skiff drift in toward its berth.

"Steve," said Sally, "please let's be careful tonight."

"Why?"

"Green called me up today. He sounded nasty. He said that he'd get you the next time you came ashore. He said every cop in the city had your description, and that they had orders to . . . to shoot to kill."

"Damn! I guess you'd better beat it, Sally. You'd better go on home and—"

"I'm in this as deep as you are, Steve." Sally's chin was firm, her gaze steady on his face.

"Okay." Steve helped her out to the dock, paid the boatman, and they went on up the gangway and made their way toward the street.

Steve hugged the shadows, and only his white-topped cap marked him there. When he reached the shore end of the dock, he was about to stride out into the thoroughfare when he stiffened and leaped back.

"What's the matter?" breathed Sally.

"There's a patrol car over there," he whispered back. "Two cops in it, and they're looking this way."

"Then they're watching the whole waterfront!"

"Probably." Steve's arctic gray eyes darted restlessly through the shadows, caught sight of an automobile ramp a half block away. "Come on."

Sally followed him closely as they passed from shadow to shadow in swift dashes. The heads in the patrol car, occasionally in plain sight, did not turn in their direction. But if a single movement caught the eyes of the law, trouble would break.

Sally, glancing over her shoulder, hurried on in Steve's wake. A series of steps were ahead, leading up to the ramp. In the busy daytime, the dock street was always too crowded with trucks and merchandise to permit the entry of passenger cars or foot traffic to the ferry building. But now the steps were deserted as was the ramp itself. Steve clattered upward.

He heard a motor's roar above him, but he did not realize what that stray car would innocently do to them. The machine turned the ramp, its headlights pointing down for an instant—and that instant was enough. Steve and Sally were caught, silhouetted in the glare. The motor roared again, the car whisked away into the fog.

Steve raced for the top, but he had already been spotted. From the police car a half block away came the order to stop.

"They'll shoot!" Sally cried.

"Come on!" Steve said sharply.

"Stop!" the officer shouted.

Almost before the mist swallowed the command, a .38 rapped its threat through the street. The slug clanged into a steel girder a split instant before Steve heard the shot. The departing yowl of the shattered bullet was like a plucked banjo string.

Steve reached back and grasped Sally's arms. He almost threw her into cover on the ramp. A second bullet twitched Steve's trouser leg. Then he was gone.

Below, the siren's wail was starting up. The patrol car's headlights swung in a circle. The machine charged for the start of the ramp.

With two hundred feet of narrow bridge on either hand, Steve despaired of making the other side. He knew that it would be impossible, even without Sally there. The car's two eyes glanced off the moisture polished girders. Steve looked down.

It was a drop of fifty feet to the street below. They were trapped on the ramp!

Suddenly Steve gathered Sally in his arms. "Hold tight to my neck!" he ordered.

With Sally clinging to him, he scrambled over the rail. He gripped two steel braces and let himself down. His hands were on the level with the sidewalk, and white with strain. Below them lay cobblestones, hard, waiting.

The headlights streaked toward them. But the car was not moving fast. The police saw that the bridge was empty, and they could not understand it. Steve could almost feel their eyes upon his hands. The machine slowed down once more.

Far off across the harbor, the *Burnham*'s brass bell clanged out four double strokes. Eight o'clock. Steve had eleven hours left of freedom—if they didn't see his hands.

A policeman's voice came to them. "They couldn't have made it, Ben."

"Yeah. It was them all right," said his companion. "Do you suppose they could have jumped the rail and—"

"Holy hell! Do you suppose they did? Turn around, let's go back!"

Gears meshed. The rear wheels of the squad car slapped against the opposite gutter. Above him Steve could see the headlights at right angles to the bridge, and he knew that those same lights were playing over his fingers! Sally's breathing was short and sibilant against his cheek.

Gears meshed again. And before Steve could realize what had taken place, the police machine was gone.

Slowly, painfully, he worked his way back up the girder and passed Sally over the edge. She tugged at his shoulders, helping him. Her face was ashen in the half-light.

"We'll have to run for it," said Steve. "They'll be back in a moment. They're down there now, looking for us. See their lights?"

"Where bound?"

"I've got to get those keys."

Sally frowned. "Isn't something else more important than that?"

"No, there isn't anything more important. See here, Sally—I didn't have a chance to tell you about the last note before we reached the dock."

"What note, Steve?"

He pulled it from his breast pocket—a ragged, tattered thing—and handed it to her.

"We'll have to be moving," he said, and followed his own suggestion by walking rapidly toward the shore side of the ramp.

Sally, watching her step with one eye and reading in the poor light with the other, gasped. "It says . . . why, it says you have to leave the brass keys on Barge Thirty between ten and midnight tonight, otherwise . . . otherwise you'll be—"

"Killed," Steve finished. "And right now we're on our way to the 'Binnacle' and Bleak Fanshaw, to get those keys. After that we'll get Andries, and after that, I hope, the murderer."

Sally gasped.

"You mean you'll give up the keys?"

Steve laughed as he headed into an alleyway and darkness. "That killer, Sally Randolph, is going to be one very surprised gentleman!"

41

CHAPTER FIVE

The Keys Draw Gunfire

T HE Binnacle was marked by a sign hanging in the dimness of an alleyway, and lit by a single blue bulb burning beneath a painted compass disc. Steve came to a halt outside the light's radius.

"Listen, Sally," he said. "I may run into trouble in here. Have you got a gun?"

"Yes, a .25 automatic. It makes more noise than it does holes."

"All right. Then get over there in that dark niche and sit tight. If you hear shouting or shooting inside, wait only a moment or two before you run for it. Is that clear?"

"Too clear, Steve."

He turned and walked to the door. Raising the latch, he pushed it back and strode in, his eyes raking the assembled sailors at the battle-scarred tables. In the fly-infested, smoke-blued interior, all eyes jerked up. Half-raised mugs of beer were lowered to the tables again, some were held motionless. A woman, her back to the entrance, started to laugh before she sensed the tightness of the room. She turned her blotchy face and stared at Steve.

Over against the wall there was a sudden movement. A man darted to his feet, eyes wide, face stolid. It was Kloss, making a dash for the door. Steve tried to stop him, but Kloss was too quick. The door slammed and he was gone.

Steve turned again to face the room. At the far end, beside a cashier's wicket, was a short bar. The fly-specked mirror behind it caught Steve's image and threw it back to him, dimmed.

Behind the cashier's wicket stood Bleak Fanshaw, a remarkably pale man in a remarkably dirty apron. His squat face was a series of sweat-beaded folds. His eyes, small and black, contracted as Steve approached him. Fanshaw glanced uneasily over his shoulder and then back at Steve.

"Hello, Fanshaw," said Steve.

"Hello." Fanshaw's voice was flat, and somehow slippery. "I don't believe—"

"You know me, all right. I'm Steve Craig."

"Oh, sure. How are you?" Fanshaw smiled, displaying time-stained teeth. "Remember you when you was a little feller. How you making out, Steve?"

"Let's go in that back room," said Steve, his face a perfect mask. "I want to ask you a few things."

"Sure, Stevie, sure. Anything I can do for you. Your dad and me were great pals—great pals. Anything I can—"

"I read some of the letters you wrote him," said Steve, flatly.

"Oh, well . . . ah . . . come in this room here, where we can talk without being disturbed."

Steve followed Bleak Fanshaw into the cubicle which served the Binnacle's proprietor as an office. A dusty, roll-top desk was against one wall, a rusty, paintless safe against the other.

Fanshaw seated himself in a swivel chair which squeaked, and waved Steve to another. Steve kept his feet.

"Listen, Fanshaw," Steve began, "to hell with lies, get me? I know that you kept some of Dad's accounts and some of his belongings, but that wasn't from Dad's choice, as I see it."

"Can I help it if Captain Jeremiah don't—didn't like my terms?"

"He owed you money, didn't he?"

"Used to. He was going to pay it up this trip. While you're here, Stevie—"

"I'm not paying off debts, Fanshaw. It wasn't enough to worry about. I don't know how all this happened, and I don't care. What did he give you as security?"

"Security?" said Fanshaw through flabby lips.

"Certainly. He gave you a ring of brass keys, didn't he? A ring of keys belonging to some Chinese chests. I want those keys."

Fanshaw smiled, and then laughed. His paunch shook under the dirty apron. "You got me all wrong, Stevie. Your dad borrowed some dollars off me when he was a boy and then forgot to pay them back. When I started to press the matter in 1910, he said he'd pay me right away, but he never did. Then he needed some more, and I let him have it. He gave me that—" Fanshaw's teeth clicked.

"That ring of keys," finished Steve. "There's your safe. The keys must be in that. Get them out, and make it fast!"

Fanshaw was smiling again. He waddled to the safe, squatted before it and pressed greasy, fat fingers to the crusty dial. The tumblers fell audibly. He swung open the door. Reaching inside, he seemed to have trouble with an inner door. Abruptly he sprang up. A large black revolver was centered on Steve's chest.

"Stay where you are!" he cried. "Don't move, or I'll shoot! Try to hold a man up, will you? You're a common thief! Boys . . . oh, boys!" he shouted. "Come back here! I got this guy. He was trying to stick me up!"

Steve backed against the wall. The office door swung back and several longshoremen and sailors crowded into the room, their eyes eager with the prospect of a fight. The blotchy-faced woman was behind them, peering curiously at Steve.

Two sailors made a grab for Steve's arms. Fanshaw backed away, lowering his gun.

Steve's voice was low, well modulated. "Stand back, buckos."

"Haw!" jeered one, and stepped in and grabbed again. Steve's fist spatted against the stubbly jaw. The man went down, eyes rolling white.

"Stand back!" repeated Steve.

A sailor shouted, and dived in. Abruptly he sprawled back over the first man. Fanshaw's gun swung up. Men pushed back away from Steve.

"You can't do that!" shrieked Bleak Fanshaw. "You can't! Hear me?"

A sailor at the door pounded away. "I'll get the cops!" he shouted over his shoulder. The front door slammed. Steve pressed the wall, watching Fanshaw.

"We'll have you out of here in a second," said Fanshaw, very brave behind his gun. "You can't come in here robbing honest men and get away with it."

Steve backed against the wall. The office door swung back and several longshoremen and sailors crowded into the room, their eyes eager with the prospect of a fight.

"I wasn't robbing you," Steve said slowly. "I want those keys, and I'll get them!"

"He'll get them!" mocked Fanshaw. "The cops will settle your hash, young feller. I hear they been looking for you right smart. I also hear there's something like a reward out for the first man that sights you on land. How do you like that? Takes the wind right out of your sails, huh?"

"Those keys aren't any good to you," said Steve. "You don't even know where the chests are."

"Don't I, though? You'd have a big surprise coming right at you, young feller. When Craig first came back—"

"Go on," Steve prompted. Fanshaw's mouth was shut tight. Steve snorted. "When Jeremiah Craig came back from the Orient, you made a demand on him for your money. How much was it?"

"Ten thousand dollars."

"That isn't so much. Why didn't he pay?"

"The customs wasn't paid on that truck he brought in, and Hawkins—" Fanshaw shut his mouth once more.

"And so he gave you the keys to keep you quiet until he could get a good assessment on the chest contents. Why weren't those chests assessed by the customs?"

Fanshaw glared.

"Because you tried to blackmail him!" snapped Steve. "Because you wouldn't give the keys back to him to have an assessment made *unless* he contracted to give you fifty percent of his share. That's why!"

"How did you know?" grated Fanshaw.

Steve grinned into the flabby face. "Because I guessed it, that's all. And I'd only have to take one look at you to be able to tell what kind of a rat you are. And now you think that Dad's death will give you full ownership because you've got the keys. You're wrong. I'm still on my two feet."

Fanshaw's eyes dilated. He glanced down at the heavy black revolver and hefted it. Turning his eyes to the men about him, he hissed, "Get out! And you don't know anything, see?"

They drifted away. One of them, the last, closed the door. Silence reigned in the outer room. Fanshaw spun the cylinder of the revolver, making certain that its chambers were filled. He hefted the gun and licked his lips.

Steve's eyes were hard and cold on Fanshaw's face. "So you wouldn't stop at killing a man to get your way clear to those chests! Are they worth that much?"

"You're an outlaw," rattled Fanshaw. "They'll never get me for killing you!" He spoke between his teeth, as though trying to reason his nerve to an unaccustomed height. The black revolver came up. Steve's eyes bored into Fanshaw's, and the revolver dropped back. Beady sweat dripped down Fanshaw's jowls. He backed away and spun the cylinder once more.

Steve advanced a step and the gun swept back into position. Fanshaw's eyes darted around the room, as though to make certain that he could escape if Steve tackled him.

"Stop!" rapped Fanshaw. The black revolver steadied. The sights were lined on Steve's forehead. Fanshaw's small black eyes were pinpoints behind it.

Steve took a deep breath. He could not make it. That was

written on Fanshaw's face. His eyes were narrowing, he was getting ready for the shot that would give him possession of the chests.

Above Fanshaw's head was a window, dirty, long, narrow. It led to a side alley. Steve gazed longingly at it, then back at the gun. Fanshaw's fingers were tightening. A siren moaned in the far distance, doubling, trebling with every second.

Abruptly the lights went out. Fanshaw shrieked and fell back against a chair. In the sudden blackness, Steve stood for an instant, surprised, undecided. The siren's wail said that the police car was in the alley.

Steve dived for the safe. His hands rattled through a drawer filled with bric-a-brac. They came into contact with keys, dozens of keys. He crammed them all into his pocket. Something else, round and splashing, was beside his foot. A can of brass polish. Steve took that, too.

Fanshaw fumbled and cursed in the blackness, reaching out with the gun muzzle. Steve went down on all fours, crawling forward. Fanshaw's legs were in his grasp, and his heavy, flabby body was across Steve's shoulders. Simultaneously, the front door exploded. Loud, excited police voices were there. Sailors yelled excitedly. Fanshaw, squirming, reached out and threw the door open. The flashlight stabbed in and bored the two on the office floor.

"It's Craig!" bellowed an officer. "Shoot!"

Steve grabbed at Fanshaw's gun, secured it, and tried to sight the flashlight which still betrayed him. Two shots racketed in opposite directions. The flash crashed to the planks. Fanshaw jerked, squealing like a stuck pig. Something hot was greasy against Steve's face. Another flashlight jumped into play. The cold white rays glanced off Fanshaw's body and then came back to Fanshaw's face. The man's throat was ripped by the policeman's bullet. A shiny pool of blood was gathering on the floor.

The narrow window crashed and Steve was gone, running down the alley, ears keyed to the sounds of pursuit. A shadow was before him—Sally. Without a word, she fell in beside him.

They slipped through three consecutive courts. Their hurrying feet spatted against cobblestones, against asphalt, against mud.

Steve drew to a panting stop along the street of docks, well hidden in shadow. "Those lights—"

"I turned them off," said Sally. "I heard the racket, and the fuse box is outside the office. I thought maybe I could— Steve! There's blood on your coat!"

"Fanshaw's, not mine," said Steve. "A cop got him with a bullet addressed to Lieutenant Craig. Nice of Fanshaw, wasn't it? The cop did it, and it's no—" But before he could go on, the fog was ripped asunder by an agonized scream!

Steve sprang forward across the slippery asphalt. His shoes thundered along the dock planking. The scream, fainter this time, sounded again.

Steve spotted the moving blur ahead of him, close to the water's edge. It was too dark to see distinctly, and a fragment of hawser almost tripped him. He rammed onward, barely able to make out the two men who struggled together before him.

Steve's hands were reaching for the first pair of shoulders

51

when the man on the outside gave a strangled cry. He rocked for an instant over the water, then plummeted out of sight. Steve was suddenly confronted by a squirming dark mass which struck him square amidships.

Before he could grip the body, a shot came from down the dock. It was a spiteful, high-pitched crack—that of a .25 automatic.

Something shattered against Steve's head. He twisted sideways. Abruptly, empty space lay beneath him. He tried to take his assailant with him, but his hands slipped. He hit the water, a stinging blow with his shoulders and was swallowed up.

But before he was under, the .25 had sounded again. Sally was up there somewhere, and with that gun in her hand she was hardly in any danger. Instead, his late assailant had certainly better watch himself.

Blowing like a porpoise, Steve struggled back above the water. His cap was floating within five feet of him, bill uppermost. He reached out and put it on.

Something else was floating near—a mass of stringy hair. Steve laid hold of it and raised the face above the surface. He could not see the features nor the expression, but there was something in the limpness of the thing which told Steve that the man was dead.

A line splashed near at hand and Sally's excited voice cried, "Steve! Step on it! The police will be here any minute!"

Stories from the Golden Age
by L. Ron Hubbard

Join the Stories from the Golden Age Book Club Today!

Yes! Sign me up for the Book Club (*check one of the following*) and each month I will receive:

○ One paperback book at $9.95 a month.
○ Or, one unabridged audiobook CD at the cost of $9.95 a month.

Book Club members get FREE SHIPPING and handling (applies to US residents only).

Name _____ (please print)

If under 18, signature of guardian _____

Address _____

City _____ State ____ ZIP ____ Telephone ____

E-mail _____

You may sign up by doing any of the following:

1. To pay by credit card go online at www.goldenagestories.com
2. Call toll-free 1-877-842-5299 or fax this card in to 1-323-466-7817
3. Send in this card with a check for the first month payable to Galaxy Press

To get a FREE Stories from the Golden Age catalog check here ○ and mail or fax in this card.

Thank you!

Subscribe today!
And get a FREE gift.

For details, go to www.goldenagestories.com.

For an up-to-date listing of available titles visit www.goldenagestories.com

Stories
from the
Golden Age
by
L. Ron Hubbard

BUSINESS REPLY MAIL

FIRST-CLASS MAIL   PERMIT NO. 75738   LOS ANGELES CA

POSTAGE WILL BE PAID BY ADDRESSEE

GOLDEN AGE BOOK CLUB
GALAXY PRESS
7051 HOLLYWOOD BLVD
LOS ANGELES CA 90028-9771

CHAPTER SIX

Caught in His Own Trap

STEVE grasped the line Sally had thrown to him. With a quick pair of half hitches he secured it under the arms of the body. Glancing toward the dock, Steve saw a set of rungs nailed against a piling. He struck out for them and in a moment he was standing beside Sally on the dock, water running from his clothes to form a small shining puddle about his soggy shoes.

Close by, a nightstick was being pounded against a sidewalk.

"The police!" Sally whispered. "Steve, let's—"

"We're cut off at the end of this dock. We'll either have to take wings and fly, or swim."

"Oh, I was a fool to fire those shots, Steve! But the thing was rushing at me and I couldn't do anything else. I didn't hit anything, but—"

"Give me a hand with this line, Sally. And take a half hitch on your nerve. That's a dead man floating down there."

Sally's hands found the rope.

Steve's shoulders braced under the strain. The limp, dangling body crept nearer to the wharf level, its head lolling back, its mouth half open.

A tug, going on a belated errand, passed near them, throwing out a glow of lights. Steve pulled the corpse over the side and laid it out. Sally, her palm against her mouth, looked away. She could see small lights bobbing on the street. The pounding of many feet was sweeping down on them.

Steve's face went white. His hands stiffened and his eyes were wide with horror.

"My God, Sally, it's Jim!"

A thin trickle of water-diluted blood was running down Jim Craig's side, from the knife wound under his left arm. Jim's hard grin was gone, and in its place was a mask of frozen surprise.

Steve snapped to his feet, stared at the lights, then looked up at the side of the warehouse. "Quick, Sally! Get up that ladder! We'll try to make it over the top to the other side!"

Sally darted for the rungs and went up. Steve looked down once more into his brother's dead face. Then he followed.

A bellow came from the dock. "Hold it there! I'll shoot!"

Steve went on up. Sally's white face was just above him.

"It's Steve Craig!" came from below.

A barrage of lead snapped spitefully at the warehouse side. Steve wavered for an instant, stopped. Something like a moan came from his throat. His hands caught at the eaves, and then Sally was pulling at his shoulders, helping him.

Steve struggled to his feet and raced up the ramp which led to the top of the sloping roof. Half sliding, half running, he went down the other side, Sally close on his heels.

Another ladder was there, and they scrambled down.

A string of barges lay between the two piers. Steve leaped to the first deck, reached up and aided Sally, and then sped away toward the far dock, going from barge to barge.

Steve's face went white. . . .
"My God, Sally, it's Jim!"

Up another ladder, and they were standing beside a second warehouse. But Steve did not slacken their pace. He made for the street, crossed it and dived into the shadows on the other side.

Not until then did he stop. He slumped against a brick wall. The exertion of lifting his head seemed too great for him.

"Steve, what's wrong?" panted Sally.

"I . . . I just got out of breath a little."

"Did they hit you?"

"Just a nick. Scraped my side. I can't . . . can't even feel it. Forget it. I'll be all right in a moment." He lifted his head and smiled reassuringly.

"This is Ship Street, Steve. Hadn't we better go up to Andries' place? They might search for us here."

Steve squared his shoulders and took her arm. His steps were exaggerated in length, his course a little wobbly. In a moment they were knocking on the door to Number Ten.

Again the face at the window, again the sliding of heavy bolts on the other side of the door. Joel Andries blinked at them.

"What's the matter?" he demanded.

Steve and Sally stepped inside. Steve fumbled for a chair and sat down. "Andries, my brother was murdered just now."

"Murdered! Who did it?" His bright eyes prodded Steve's face.

"I'm sure I don't know, but I'll have an idea very shortly. Andries, I received a note saying that I was to be at Barge Thirty between ten and midnight, and that I was to leave a ring of brass keys there."

"Brass keys!"

"Did you ever hear of my dad owning any that were valuable?"

"What's a string of brass keys got to do with this?"

"I'm sure I don't know."

Andries limped away and took down a dark jacket from its hook on the wall. "I'll go with you, Steve. And I'll take me a blackjack and some brass knuckles along. We'll nail this gent and get everything straight. Did you say you had those keys to leave as bait?"

"Yes, I've got them in my pocket," Steve replied.

"All right," said Andries, shrugging into the jacket. "We'll leave the keys in plain sight on the barge deck. I know just where that barge is. There isn't much light there, but the keys are bound to shine a little, so you hide yourself on the barge and I'll hide behind a bitt on the dock. And when somebody comes along to pick up the keys, we'll both jump him. If he gets away from you, I'll rap him good and plenty."

"That's a good plan," Sally agreed. "I'll hide—"

Andries shook his head. "No, sir, miss. You better stay right here and wait for us. There's apt to be a lot of bloodshed and I don't want to have to worry about you."

"He's right, Sally," said Steve. "You stay here and rest up. It's been a pretty tough evening for you."

Sally frowned, then reluctantly agreed.

"Now," said Andries, "what about this murder of your brother? Got any ideas why he was killed?"

"None at all. All I know is that the police spotted me on the scene of the crime. They'll try to make out that I did this killing, and the first too."

"They spotted you!" wheezed Andries. "That's bad, Steve. They saw your face?"

"By the flashlights."

"No way to get out of that," Andries sighed. "If you were there with a dead man and the police saw you and didn't see anyone else, then you're the bucko that will have to take the blame."

A decanter of West Indies rum stood on the dusty table. Steve poured out a glass and downed it. "That's better. Let's get going, Andries. It's after ten now."

Andries pulled a weather-beaten hat down over his head and opened the door. "You wait right there, Miss Sally. We'll be back, and we'll bring you the killer to boot."

Steve followed the limping old man out into the damp mist.

They walked slowly. Andries' peg leg rapped monotonously on the pavement as he hitched along.

"I don't like this fog," he volunteered after minutes of silence. "It hurts my stump somehow. I'm going to get out of this place some day. I'll go back up over the mountains where it's dry and warm all the time."

"Hope you can, Andries."

"That's Barge Thirty up ahead. It's an oil barge, and it's empty. Hasn't been used for quite a while, either, so there's no watchman hanging around it. It's pretty dirty."

"That's all right," said Steve. "I meant to tip Hawkins off that the keys would be there, but I didn't have time, and if he's the one, it won't be necessary. He seems—whoever *he* is—pretty anxious to get this set of keys."

"Here we are. You just drop down on that deck. Can you see?"

"Not very well. It's pretty black."

Andries grunted. "I've seen blacker places than this. That coil of rope down there ought to be a good place to hide. You can just climb inside it, and then whatever way this feller comes from, you'll be hid. And you just drop those keys out in front of you where they'll be in easy reach. I'll hide myself up here on the water side of this bitt."

Steve lowered himself to the barge, wincing as he twisted his side. His wet shoes stuck in the thick tar on the deck as he walked. With his hands he found the coil of rope, a neat pile, hollow in the center—a perfect barricade. Steve slid into the middle and sat down, listening. He heard nothing except the night noises—the water lapping under a pier, the far away clatter of a street car, a subdued thunder of winches and booms where a ship was loading or unloading.

Satisfied that he had not been observed, Steve climbed to his feet. He took out his handkerchief and held it over the deck before him. The sparkling mass of keys jangled as they struck the tarred surface. As he sank back, he had the uncanny feeling that he was being watched.

If they had seen him, thought Steve, they could certainly make short work of him in his present cramped position. He had to rely on the fact that they—or he—had not noticed him. Parting some of the strands, Steve saw that an anchored ship out in the harbor was partially lit up. That would have silhouetted him from shore.

Minutes passed. The fog crept in through Steve's wet clothes and chilled him. Now that he could not move about, he realized how stiff and cold he was. He heard the *Burnham's* bell sound six times—eleven o'clock. The sound made him lonesome. Billy Reynolds would be tramping up and down the steel deck, keeping warm, waiting for him to come back.

Down in the wardroom the radio would be going and a game of poker would be in progress. Steve corrected that. Only the chief engineer and the skipper would be aboard, besides Billy Reynolds. And that thought led to the short-handedness of the destroyer. They'd be a weary crew by the time they got to Guantánamo, if he wasn't there to stand his watch. The thought made Steve squirm restlessly. If he didn't get everything straight, he'd be in a jail cell looking out through the bars.

The far-off ship's bell clanged seven times—eleven-thirty. Steve wished the fellow would come, if he was coming at all.

Andries' cautious voice came from the dock. "All right, Steve?"

"All right."

Steve was tired. He caught his head nodding. He twisted into another position.

Then he sat up straight with a jerk. He thought he had heard a footfall on the other end of the barge. His fists clenched, and he prepared to lunge out if anyone came near the keys. Raising his head a little, he could see the keys sparkling—the only distinct things in all this blackness.

Thinking he had been mistaken, Steve sank back on his heels, and fell to pondering on why his father and then his brother had been killed. He had an annoying hunch that he had all the facts right there in the palm of his hand, but couldn't put them together properly. He wished someone would come for those keys. He couldn't remember when he had been so miserably cold.

He wondered how Sally was taking it. She hadn't bargained for all this when she had said "yes." It had seemed so simple at the time. All he had to do was buy a license and a ticket for her to Guantánamo, and they'd sail away to a tropical clime. It had sounded too good to be true. He smiled as he thought how well Sally had stood by him.

He sat up once more, blinking. He had heard a footstep—he was certain of it this time. He leaned a little way out of the coil and glanced around. Suddenly he remembered that the ship out there would silhouette him with its dim lights. He jerked back, listening.

Abruptly something rustled at his back. Steve stared up. A moving blur was over his head—something shiny was coming down. His hands, as he raised them to ward off the blow, felt as though they had never moved before. His ears caught the swish of the blunt instrument. It seemed to come down forever before it hit him.

Light exploded in his brain. He felt great cogwheels clicking over inside him. He was trying to swim out of black depths. Suddenly he let go all holds and sank back into the coil, his head lolling back.

His cap rolled away, a small white blur in the darkness. The sea-tarnished spread eagle was down in the tar. A heavy foot stepped on the cap bill, cracking it. . . .

CHAPTER SEVEN

Menace Strikes from the Dark

STEVE struggled back through layer after layer of gauze, each one a little less black than the last. Finally the gauze dissolved itself into fog and dark dampness. He put out his hand and felt about him, encountering the ropes. Gingerly, he felt of the top of his skull. He was sick and cold and stiff, but he made himself stand up.

As soon as he made a sound, Andries' voice floated down to him from the dock. "See anything yet, Steve?"

Steve exploded. "You're a hell of a guard!" Then he realized that it wasn't Andries' fault. "Somebody sneaked up on me and slugged me."

"They did!" Andries scurried to the edge of the dock and helped Steve up to his own level. "I never heard a thing! They must have dropped onto the back of the barge and sneaked up. Every time you bobbed your head up, Steve, you might have been seen."

Steve shook the numbness out of his brain. "Where are the keys?" He jumped back to the barge deck. Andries, grumbling, also came down. Steve was fumbling on the tarred deck.

"Gone?"

"Gone!" said Steve, disgustedly. He retrieved his cap and set it on his head. Then, feeling suddenly weak, he sat down on the coil.

"Listen, Steve," said Andries. "I'm going to locate Hawkins and Kloss, and I'm going to find out where they were this last hour. They're not going to get away with slugging you and stealing those keys!"

"All right," Steve said. "You go ahead. I'll go back and get Sally."

"You're not coming with me?"

Steve shook his aching head. "No. We might as well divide up forces. You see Hawkins, if you can locate him. I'll go on the scout for something else. All right?"

"Sure," said Andries. He struggled up the dockside and hobbled away, his peg leg thumping in agitated tempo.

When the wave of sickness was gone, Steve felt in his pocket for his cigarette lighter. Being a wise sailor, he kept his smokes in a watertight case and did not depend upon matches. Lighting the smoke, he sat regarding the glowing spark and thinking.

Presently he ignited the lighter again and got down on his hands and knees, examining the barge deck. The imprint of the keys was still there in the tar. Steve crawled in a small circle until the lighter grew hot to his touch.

He stood up with an angry exclamation and headed down the dock, walking fast. He tried to spot a taxi along the main thoroughfare, but was unsuccessful. He struck out as fast as he could for Ship Street, his brows puckered in a worried frown.

Ship Street was in silence when he reached it. Two lights were showing, and one of them came from the window of Number Ten. Steve, with half a block to go, stopped dead still. His eyes lighted up with surprise.

From behind him came the moaning wail of a siren and the racketing chuckle of a police exhaust whistle. He started to run toward Number Ten. Headlights swept around the corner, and he saw that he could not make it.

Despairingly, he plunged into a dark entrance and hugged the wall. The police cars drew up with squealing brakes before Number Ten. Men with riot guns in their hands swarmed out.

Detective-Sergeant Green, cigar glowing in the fog, bellowed, "Break the door down! In and get him!"

Two brawny officers dashed up the steps and threw their shoulders into the door. It creaked. They lunged again. With the crash of splintering bolts, the door flew wide. The police swept in like an avalanche.

Their cries were suddenly still, and for a moment all was tomblike on Ship Street. Then Detective-Sergeant Green came out, pulling Sally Randolph by the arm.

"Come on now, Miss Randolph," rumbled Green. "He's hiding in there somewhere and you'll save the boys a lot of trouble if you tell them where."

"He isn't in there!" Sally flared. "Let me go!"

From inside came the sounds of pounding feet. The police were thoroughly wrecking Andries' house in their search. It was characteristic of the neighborhood that neither heads nor lights showed in nearby windows.

Haggarty came out, puffing. "He isn't in there, Green. We searched the place from top to bottom."

"Then he's somewhere around here. Search the streets!"

Steve pressed back against the wall. He was in a blind alley and there was no escape.

Haggarty, still puffing, said, "No use of that. He's blocks away by this time."

"You can't hold me!" cried Sally. "I'll—"

"You'll what?" said Green. "You're under arrest as an accomplice to the murder of Jim Craig. We got the goods on you."

"You're lying."

"Yeah? Well, here's a warrant for your arrest. Take a peep at that. Everything's regular, see? Everything. And when we get your boyfriend, the elusive lieutenant, he'll have company in jail."

Steve bristled and hugged back against the wet bricks.

"He's not around. We didn't get a thing."

"The hell we didn't, Haggarty," snapped Green. "We got his girl. And he'll turn himself in to get her out. That's all I want. That's every bit that I want. And she'll squeal when we get her under the lights. Won't you, lady?"

"You'll get nothing out of me, Detective-Sergeant Green. Men as brave as you ought to get medals as big as dinner plates for their courage, and keep your hands off me!"

"Huh!" commented Green. "Haggarty, see that a couple men are posted around here, in case our pal comes back. If you guys hadn't been so slow on this, we'd have had him. Trust you to—"

"Aw, we came as fast as we could," said a patrolman, stalking out to his car. "If there were two ounces of brains in the detective force—"

"Shut up!" Green barked. "And you can drive me and this girl back to headquarters."

The cars got under way one by one, and in a few moments the street was deserted. From behind the door of Number Ten came the glint of a drawn revolver. They were waiting up there.

Steve, eyes cold with anger, slipped silently out of his hiding place and sprinted for the waterfront.

Wishing that he knew where Andries had gone, he stood back from a street lamp and gazed about him. Remembering his earlier plan, he reached into his pocket and drew forth the warehouse receipt he had found in Captain Craig's effects.

Water-soaked and limp, the paper was hard to read. He took off his cap, laid the receipt on the flat white top and moved nearer the lamp.

Glancing up at the black painted number on the dock across the street, he turned and headed north, walking in the shadows, avoiding any contact with people walking along the thoroughfare—an easy feat, for the thoroughfare was almost deserted.

He passed a door from whence came the jangle of a mechanical piano and the shrill voice of a woman singer. Bottles crashed within, someone swore. The place was silent for a brief pause. Then the mechanical piano was fed another nickel and the woman sang once more. A seaman lurched through the swinging door, fumbled for the sidewalk with his feet and continued up the street, away from Steve.

When Steve had gone a hundred feet beyond this strip of light, another seaman came out. He studied Steve's retreating back an instant, then turned and lumbered up an alley, muttering under his breath.

Steve watched the pier numbers as they went by. They were hard to make out on the dimmed buildings, and he was forced to pause occasionally to reassure himself that he had not passed the dock he wanted. The cobblestones were slippery under his shoes.

Ahead, in a pier office, a light was swinging back and forth as though it had just been lit. Beyond it Steve saw a man leaning over a roll-top desk.

Steve quickened his pace. This was the dock he sought. From somewhere near came the sputter of a launch motor. Steve paid it no heed.

He stepped to the office door, gripped the knob and strode in. Brant Hawkins jumped away from the desk. The German sailor, Kloss, whirled about, his breathing loud in the otherwise silent room.

"Where are they?" snapped Steve.

"What?" Hawkins demanded, his face paling.

"The keys! Where are they?"

"I don't know anything about keys," Hawkins whined.

"Shall I throw him out?" rumbled Kloss.

"Try it," invited Steve, hopefully.

Hawkins' hand was inching toward the desk drawer. With a sudden lunge, Steve went over the side of the roll-top desk and came up, holding a .38 police revolver in his hand.

Hawkins blinked, shifted uneasily in his chair. His wing collar was slightly wilted, his usually shaven jaw was covered by a blue-black stubble.

"You better watch out," said Kloss, staring at the gun.

"Put it away," Hawkins pleaded.

"Yes?" said Steve. "And then what would you do? Pardon me, but I'd like to use your phone."

"Phone!" Hawkins said. "Who you going to call?"

"The police."

"Say!" said Kloss. "You don't want—"

Hawkins rapped the top of his desk with his fingers. "Can't we talk this thing over, Lieutenant Craig? If you were to name your price—"

Kloss, hands clenched, had better ideas. He started to lean forward. Steve reached out with his gun and rapped Kloss' knuckles.

Reaching for the phone, Steve lifted the receiver. "Give me police headquarters, central."

"Now wait!" pleaded Hawkins. "There isn't any use in—"

"Hello, desk? Give me Sergeant Green's office, please."

Hawkins ran a finger under his collar. "What are you going to do, Lieutenant?"

"Call the police in on this."

"But, Lieutenant, there isn't any use in— Wait a minute! Hang up, will you?"

Steve heard Green's hello at the other end. "Hello, Green? This is Lieutenant Craig speaking, yes, Lieutenant Craig. Listen a moment, will you? Bring your gang down here to Pier Thirty-four. Pier Thirty-four, that's right. . . . You've got cast-iron nerve yourself. And don't be all day. And don't forget to bring Miss Randolph."

"That's that," said Steve, hanging up.

From the expression on his face, neither Hawkins nor Kloss could suspect the anxiety behind the mask. Steve knew that he had settled nothing so far. He took the water-soaked blue receipt out of his pocket and placed it on Hawkins' desk.

"Where is this stuff?" he demanded.

Hawkins eyed the receipt, frowning. "In the sail loft, Lieutenant. All the way back. It belongs . . . it belongs to Jeremiah Craig . . . it did, I mean."

Steve's back was partially turned to Kloss, and Kloss took advantage of the fact. He aimed a kick at Steve's gun and sent it spinning into the corner. Then he raced out of the office, and before Steve could move, Hawkins had pounded out in Kloss' wake.

Steve shook his numb wrist and picked up the .38. He could hear the two running inside the warehouse, and he darted after them.

Hawkins' legs were disappearing up the ladder into the sail loft. Kloss was already out of sight. Lights glowed on the first floor of the warehouse, but all was darkness above.

Steve looked for the switch, found it, and shut it off. Then he groped for the steep ladder and began the ascent as silently as possible. He did not intend to be slugged a second time that night, but he knew that he was risking just that.

A rung at a time, he made his way, gripping the .38. The tar on his shoes—the tar from the barge—made a small sound each time he lifted a foot. No sound came from overhead. They were waiting for him.

Near at hand, Steve could hear the sputter and cough of a launch engine. He wondered if it were a police patrol boat.

The square opening was close to his head. He reached out and felt for a clear space on which to step. His hand encountered no obstacles. Moving as slowly as possible, he drew himself over the edge and lay flat on his face, listening.

A rustling sound came from one end of the garretlike place. Steve hitched himself toward it across the dusty floor. To his right he could see a square of dim light. That meant that the loft had a large, glassless window facing the bay.

Something rolled under his hand, and the noise was like thunder in his ears. A flashlight jabbed at him, holding him in its bright glare. Steve shot at the light. The echo of the sound rolled back and forth through the emptiness. The light went out.

A ribbon of flame came from another quarter. Steve scurried for cover. A pile of canvas lay between him and the lighted square. Having no other choice, he shot in behind it.

A bullet thumped into the heavy fabric. Another threw up a shower of splinters from the floor. Suddenly all was still again. The sputtering engine of the launch seemed louder to Steve. He risked making a target out of himself by crawling over to the window and looking down.

Of the launch he could only see a line of sparks from the exhaust. But these lay directly under the opening. In front of Steve was a makeshift hoist without any line.

Something bumped Steve's foot. He leaped aside and felt quickly about him. The canvas pile had moved!

Steve understood then what was happening. They were trying to shove this pile out the window. And if they succeeded, he would be shoved into empty space. If there was only water below, it would be all right. But that launch would break him into bits before he could know what he hit.

He tried to scramble up over the pile. A shot met him, scorching his cheek. He had evidently exposed himself against the lighted square. The pile moved again, and now he was barely a foot from the brink.

The foot narrowed down to six inches, the six inches to one. Steve was hanging over the edge. He loosed his hold on the canvas and grabbed for the ledge. His entire length dangled over nothing. The sputtering launch was directly below.

Expecting to see the canvas pile crash on him and knock him loose any second, Steve heard a scurry of footsteps within the loft. A strangled voice swore. Feet pounded across the planking.

Puzzled, Steve could only hang on, and hope that Green would come before the men in the loft would remember him and come back to knock off the bolts of goods. Experimentally he tried to pull himself up on the pile again, but the cloth slid toward him. The leaning tower over his head tilted perilously.

CHAPTER EIGHT

Jeremiah Craig Is Avenged

FIVE minutes later, the wail of sirens came from the front of the wharf. Feet pounded planks in the loft. Brakes screeched. The ladder to the sail loft creaked with the weight of many men.

A prayer was on Steve's lips. If everything did not turn out all right, he would be jailward bound. If he could not satisfy Green of the murderer's identity, he would have to stand the charges himself. And if he could not hold on for another couple minutes, he would have to worry no more.

A shot racketed through the warehouse. Green's voice was bellowing at everything, everyone. Police shouted orders which went unheard in the din. Several shots came close together.

Abruptly everything was silent. A light showed itself on the other side of the canvas pile.

Steve shouted, "Hey, in there! Move this canvas, will you?"

Grunts sounded, and the canvas began to move. Hands were under Steve's arms pulling him up. Badges glittered everywhere.

Steve's first glance around halted upon Sally Randolph. She stood at the top of the loft ladder, police close by. Steve tried to smile at her.

Green's hard tones fell upon Steve's ears. "Well, we've got you!"

"I called you here!" said Steve.

"Turned yellow, huh?" snapped Green.

Steve looked around and saw Hawkins and Kloss. They stood close together, handcuffed. Steve's eyes fell on Andries.

Andries nodded brightly. "We got 'em all right!" he crowed.

Steve looked up at Green and then leaned back on his improvised canvas chair. "Green, you're a fair man—I've always heard that about you."

Detective-Sergeant Green was somewhat taken aback. "Well," he said, taking his cigar out of his mouth and rolling it between his fingers, "there are those that say so."

"All right, then. You found some brass keys on the prisoners, didn't you?"

"No, but we can look. Hey, Haggarty, search those two mugs, will you?"

"Don't let him touch the keys with his bare hands," Steve cautioned.

"Sure, I get it! Fingerprints."

Haggarty turned Hawkins and Kloss around. From the left pocket of Hawkins' coat came a jingle. With his handkerchief Haggarty reached into the pocket and brought forth a set of keys.

"There," said Steve. "Now listen to me, Hawkins. What were you and Kloss trying to smuggle on Dad's ships?"

Hawkins turned pale and glanced hurriedly toward the back of the loft. Green, catching on, went to the rear, pulled up a tarpaulin and uncovered a pile of cases.

"Rum," said Green. "What's this all about? Hasn't repeal done away with you smugglers yet?"

"Well, you see," faltered Hawkins, "the tax—"

"Oh, so you make the tax off it!" said Green. He saw that one of the cases was open, and with a quick glance about him he grinned and took out a bottle. "Well, this doesn't happen to be in my jurisdiction," he said, "but I'll fine you a quart."

"All right," said Steve. "Now see that pile of chests over there?"

"Where?" asked Green. "Oh, yeah. Chinese chests. What about 'em?"

"I want you to open them up," said Steve.

"Okay." Green reached for the brass keys Haggarty held in the handkerchief.

"No," said Steve. "Those won't fit it. They came out of Bleak Fanshaw's souvenirs. Here's the real bunch." He pulled a ring from his breast pocket and jangled it. The keys were dull, unwieldy.

Green took the keys and approached the chests, inserting one after another into the first lock, until he found one that would fit. It was easy to see by his actions that he was humoring Steve Craig.

The first chest came open. An officer threw a flash into it. Green stepped back, his jaw slackened. "Why, the thing's filled with brocades!" He picked one up, handling it carefully. Then he reached in and found a small box. Opening it, he exposed the contents to the flashlight. With an appreciative exclamation he drew out a string of pearls.

"Huh!" said Green. "You mean all six of these chests are full of such stuff? Why was it left here?"

"Because," explained Steve, "even the king of safecrackers couldn't make a dent in those metal-bound chests. And unless they were opened and the contents moved, it would take a big crew of men to steal one. That's Jeremiah Craig's share of the loot of a Chinese junk he took out in the Yellow Sea."

"China Sea!" snapped Andries.

"Yellow Sea," repeated Steve. "Now listen, Green—did you pick up anyone loitering about the dock?"

"Sure. Say, Craig, you must know all the answers!" Green shouted down the ladder. "Hey! Bring that guy up here!"

"All right," Steve continued. "Green, all this was done to get possession of the set of keys I just handed over to you."

"Yeah?" said Green.

"Yeah," Steve repeated. "You can check all my statements by calling up Bleak Fanshaw—and several others. Green, I received a note this afternoon. You've got it, haven't you, Sally?"

"He took it," said Sally, pointing to Green.

Green nodded. "Yeah. That bunk about you leaving the keys on the barge. Well, what about it?"

"I left the keys there. Or at least," amended Steve, "I left a set of keys out there. Bleak Fanshaw lent them to me. And I had him shine them up with liquid brass polish."

"I get it," said Green. "Liquid polish leaves a dry surface. And fingers leave prints in the form of corrosion. But get on, Craig. I'm doing you a hell of a big favor by listening to you at all. This stuff has started to look kind of screwy."

"Well, you'll find the print on those keys," said Steve.

Green reached into his overcoat and drew out an old envelope. Then he unscrewed the top of his fountain pen and approached Hawkins.

"Here you go, rummy," said Green. He smeared ink on the index finger of Hawkins' hand and took the print off with the envelope. Then he did the same with the other fingers. Finally he turned to Kloss and repeated the trick.

Approaching a policeman with an electric lantern, Green took the keys he had found on Hawkins and compared the prints. He jerked his head at Steve.

"They aren't the ones, are they?" said Steve.

"No!" cried Green. "But how did you know that?"

"Just did, that's all. Here, look at my hat. See the underside of the cover?"

"Sure. It's got a round black spot."

"That's right," said Steve. "That's a footprint left there by Joel Andries. Joel Andries is the murderer of Jeremiah Craig and my brother Jim!"

Andries jumped back, his peg leg rapping the planks. He scowled. Green, sudden comprehension on his face, headed for him, fountain pen and envelope ready.

"No!" cried Andries. "No!"

Green grabbed the flailing arms and obtained the prints. Then he compared them with those on the key. He smiled at Steve. "They're the same!"

"Sure they are. Andries was up here before Hawkins came. And Andries didn't want those keys to be found on him, so he planted them on Hawkins. Simple enough. It was Andries who tipped you off where to find me, wasn't it? He said to go to Number Ten Ship Street. Well, that's his own place. He knew I was going back for Sally. He thought I'd run into you. You'd run me in, and that would be that!"

Andries was squirming in the long arm of the law. His eyes were glaring, his mouth tight. "I'll get you yet, Steve Craig! I said I'd get all of you, and I will!"

"Maybe so," said Steve. "But I don't believe in ghosts, get me?"

"Anyway, it sounds good," Green conceded.

"Yes, it does. Andries was with Dad out in China, on the *Mary Anne*. When they were in the Yellow Sea they were attacked by pirates, but they overcame the pirates and looted the junk of these chests.

"Andries was not satisfied with the division that Captain Craig wanted to make, and led a mutiny against my father. Evidently, the mutiny was put down and Andries was punished by—"

"Keelhauled!" cried Andries. "Do you hear me? Keelhauled! They passed ropes over my wrists and under the hull, and pulled me all the way through!"

Steve cut in on the ranting. "So a shark or something of the sort nailed him while he was in the water. He pleaded he'd behave, and Dad didn't report the matter, thinking that Andries had suffered enough.

"But all these years Andries has nursed a grudge against the Craigs. He killed Jeremiah Craig because he thought Jeremiah Craig had these brass keys in his personal possession. Then he threw the body in the water downstream from the destroyer. Finally he waited until I came up the waterfront with Sally Randolph. Then, being certain that I was near to take the blame, he knifed my brother.

"But Andries did not want to kill me. He cooked up this barge idea. He was to watch on the dock, and I was to watch on the barge. He slugged me from behind, took these keys, informed you where you could find me, and then lit out for this place. He was at work trying to open the chests with the wrong keys when I got here.

"Hawkins and Kloss had been running this minor smuggling racket, and hearing about this murder business, they were afraid that they would be exposed. Their crime was small but it seemed big to them. I believe the fine is only a couple hundred dollars in their case.

"I figured most of this out when I saw this round black spot in my cap. I picked this cap up before Andries hit the barge. Therefore Andries had to be on the barge before I came to, and he acted as though he didn't even know I'd been slugged.

"Further, I was puzzled as to why the man who slugged me had not killed me outright. It could have been done easily enough. Andries hadn't killed me because he wanted to get the loot and let me take the rap for both murders."

"Wait a minute!" said Green. "How did Andries know all your movements?"

"Brought that man up yet?" said Steve. "Oh, there he is!"

The boatman stood woodenly at the top of the ladder.

"This is the man Sally employed to row us," Steve said. "Who recommended him to you, Sally?"

"Why . . . why, Andries did!"

"There you are," said Steve. "The boatman was to get a

launch and wait for him underneath the sail loft window of this pier. Andries was going to pass this loot down, a bale at a time. That's why he had to have the keys. And he couldn't move those chests alone—or even with ten men."

Andries was still glaring. He tried to lunge forward, but the policeman held him securely. "I'll get you for this, Craig! I'll get you! After I'd worked and slaved for years to get this all figured! And after I'd waited for months to get all three of you Craigs in port at the same time—"

"Take him away!" snapped Green. "It's open and shut, Haggarty. Take those bracelets off this guy Hawkins and his pal. We'll forget about that rum—can't be bothered with small stuff. As for you, Craig, you can be damned glad I don't jump at conclusions, see?"

"I'm glad you don't," said Steve. He went across the planking and took Sally's hand. Big tears stood in her eyes. Her lips were trembling. Steve stopped that.

"We'd better go home and get some sleep—both of us, Sally," he said. "After all, this is your wedding day."

"You mean everything's all right?" she asked shakily.

"Everything. And you see those chests over there? They're a wedding present that Jeremiah Craig brought you all the way from China."

She buried her face in his very much abused uniform jacket. "Oh, Steve!" she whispered.

Story Preview

NOW that you've just ventured through one of the captivating tales in the Stories from the Golden Age collection by L. Ron Hubbard, turn the page and enjoy a preview of *The Slickers*. Join hard-edged Sheriff Tex Larimee as he strides boots-first into the dangerous snare of a frame-up. When Tex arrives in the big city to help a friend, he ends up having to solve the friend's murder or be strung up himself!

The Slickers

TEX LARIMEE inserted his cigar below his scraggly mustaches and looked sideways at the stranger.

"Yep," said Tex, "I'm on my way to New York, and I'm here to tell you right now that if any of these greenhorns tries to pull anything on Tex Larimee, they'll have to talk it over with Judge Colt first."

He patted the bulge under his coat and, in doing so, displayed his bright sheriff's badge to momentary view.

The stranger tilted his bowler hat and suppressed a smile with his hand. The stranger had a diamond on his finger which matched the glitter of his hard eyes.

Tex, supposing that this partner in the smoking car had come there by chance, talked on.

"Old John Temple knows where to go for help," said Tex, nodding his head vigorously and gnawing harder on the mangled cigar. "He wouldn't trust none of those city dicks. He sent right out to Arizony for his old friend Tex Larimee."

"Who's John Temple?" said the stranger.

"What," said Tex, "you ain't never heard of John Temple? Why, snap my suspenders, but you Easterners are the most ignorant . . .Well, he's the biggest copper man in Arizony, that's what. He's got more millions than you got whiskers.

He's so rich he uses solid gold cuspidors, that's what. An' you never heard of him."

"Huh-uh," lied the stranger, fingering the diamond. "What'd he send for you for?"

"Why, to guard him, o'course. Out in Arizony, a man don't need no guardin'. Why, you could leave a million dollars sittin' in the middle of the street and nobody would think of packin' it off. But New York—wal, that's different. They'd slit your throat for a nickel in that town, I hear. John Temple, he ain't in such very good health and he wanted me to come East and bring him back home. And here I am."

"You're sheriff out there or something, aren't you?" said the stranger.

"Sure . . . Say, how'd you know?"

"Oh, you just look like a sheriff, that's all. I could spot your kind most anyplace. Big black hat, gray mustaches, high-heeled boots . . . Sure, I know your kind when I see one."

"Sheriff of Cactus County," said Tex, proudly. "Been sheriff for thirty years and they don't show no signs of kickin' me out yet."

The stranger got up and elaborately stretched. "We're passing Newark," he said. "I think I'll go get my baggage together. See you later, Sheriff."

"S'long," said Tex, looking out of the window.

The stranger went up the aisle, opened a door and passed into the next car. He promptly collared a porter and thrust a five-dollar bill into his hand. "Here, take this telegram and send it when we stop at Newark, understand?"

Tex was uncomfortable sitting on the red plush. He squirmed and shifted his gun into an easier position. He looked at the maze of chimneys which went sailing past and shook his head.

"Beats hell," said Tex. "Ain't even room to breathe out this way. No wonder John Temple wants to go home."

A few minutes later, after the stop at Newark, the train screeched to a stop in Pennsylvania Station. Tex picked up his paper suitcase and followed the other passengers down to the platform. Suspiciously, he thrust away the redcaps.

"Beats hell," said Tex. "These here Easterners ain't even strong enough to carry their own suitcases."

Disgustedly he stalked up the iron steps to the waiting room, intending to phone John Temple at the Manhattan Hotel.

The crowd was thick and noisy. Tex Larimee, standing a head taller than most of the men, gouged his way through the press, eyes yearningly fixed on the red-and-gold sign far away which said "Phones."

"Beats hell," said Tex. "Regular damned stampede."

A sallow-faced man was coming the other way. His face was thinner than a knife blade and his eyes were hot. He ran squarely into Tex. The press of the crowd held him there for a moment.

Tex shoved him away but the man was hurled back at him again.

"Doggone," said Tex, "you can't walk through me. What do you think I am? A shadow?"

The sallow-faced one drifted out and away and Tex lost

sight of him. Presently the crowd thinned and Tex made his way toward the phone signs.

He leaned over the switchboard desk. "Please, ma'am, would you call up the Manhattan Hotel for me?"

The girl glanced up, startled by the mustaches and the big black hat. "Five cents, please."

Confidently, Tex reached into his pocket. He scowled and tried another. He set down the suitcase and rapidly searched through his coat.

A baffled expression came over his leathery face. "Beats hell. I put that wallet right there in my hip pocket and I . . ."

"Five cents, please," said the girl in a mechanical voice.

Tex repeated the search and then it began to dawn upon him that he had been robbed. Hastily he felt for his gun. It was gone. He grabbed for his star and clutched nothing but vest cloth.

The girl frowned and held her earphones on tight. A policeman came up and motioned with his stick. "Move along, buddy."

"Look here," said Tex, looking earnestly at the beefy red face before him, "I'm Sheriff Tex Larimee of Cactus County, Arizony. I—"

"That so?" said the cop. "Move along, buddy, before I have to get tough with you."

"Tough with me?" said Tex, backing off to give himself arm room. "Look here, you shorthorn, when you bark at me—"

"Move along," said the cop.

A thin finger tapped the sheriff's shoulder. Full of fight,

Tex whirled and found himself facing the stranger he had met on the smoking car.

"Having trouble?" asked the man in the bowler hat.

"I been robbed," cried Tex. "I was coming through that crowd and some sticky-fingered coyote went through me like a bullet through butter. And then this blankety-blank beef steer—"

"What's that?" said the officer, juggling his nightstick.

"You heard it!" roared Tex.

Nervously, the stranger tugged at the sheriff's arm. "You better come along with me, mister. It won't do you any good to buck the law."

Tex picked up the paper suitcase and, still growling, followed his newfound friend out of the station and into the din of Seventh Avenue.

"We better have a drink," said the stranger, tipping the bowler hat forward on his milk-white brow.

Tex yelled, "All right, but I've got to call the Manhattan Hotel."

"Call from the bar," said the stranger.

Overawed by the hurry and bustle and noise, feeling small in this dingy canyon of buildings, Tex tagged along, high-heel boots scuffing the pavement, spur rowels whizzing.

They entered a small barroom on Thirty-fourth Street, where the stranger seemed to be known.

"Better go into the back room," said the stranger. "More quiet back there."

Tex was still too worried about his money and papers to

protest and he stepped through the door. The place was dimly lighted and poorly furnished with scarred tables and unpainted chairs.

A sleek-headed waiter took their order and slipped out with it.

"What the hell's the matter with people in this town?" said Tex. "They stare at you like you was something out of a museum." He gave his big black hat a defiant tug and then straightened his mustache. "I don't think I like this place. All my life I wanted to see New York and now I'm here, to hell with it."

"Oh, you have to get used to it," said the stranger.

"I don't think I'd live long enough," said Tex, "what with all them taxis scootin' around. Them drivers act like they was breakin' broncs. Where's the phone around here?"

Tex started to get up. A chilly voice behind him said, "Don't move, Bronson, and that goes for you, too, old-timer."

Tex turned carefully around. He knew that tone of voice. A man had slipped into the door and stood with his back to it holding a .45 automatic carelessly pointed in the general direction of the table. The fellow wore a checkered suit and a flaming red tie. His nose had been broken back against his face and his mouth was an ink mark across his off-side jaw.

To find out more about *The Slickers* and how you can obtain your copy, go to www.goldenagestories.com.

Glossary

STORIES FROM THE GOLDEN AGE *reflect the words and expressions used in the 1930s and 1940s, adding unique flavor and authenticity to the tales. While a character's speech may often reflect regional origins, it also can convey attitudes common in the day. So that readers can better grasp such cultural and historical terms, uncommon words or expressions of the era, the following glossary has been provided.*

bales: large bundles or packages prepared for shipping, storage, etc.

belay: stop.

belaying pin: a large wooden or metal pin that fits into a hole in a rail on a ship or boat, and to which a rope can be fastened.

bells: the strokes on a ship's bell, every half-hour, to mark the passage of time.

Binnacle: a built-in housing for a ship's compass. Used here as the name of a flophouse.

blackjack: a short, leather-covered club, consisting of a heavy head on a flexible handle, used as a weapon.

bluecoats: policemen.

bowler: derby; a hard felt hat with a rounded crown and narrow brim, created by James Lock & Co, a firm founded in 1676 in London. The prototype was made in 1850 for a customer of Lock's by Thomas and William Bowler, hat makers in Southwark, England. At first it was dubbed the *iron hat* because it was hard enough to protect the head, and later picked up the name *bowler* because of its makers' family name. In the US it became known as a *derby* from its association with the Kentucky Derby.

bracelets: a pair of handcuffs.

bucko: 1. a person who is domineering and bullying. 2. young fellow; chap; young companion.

camphor: camphor laurel; a large ornamental evergreen tree, native to Taiwan, Japan and some parts of China. It grows up to seventy feet tall and has leaves with a glossy, waxy appearance.

cargo boom: a long pole extending upward at an angle from the mast used to load and unload goods.

carronades: short cast-iron cannons. With their low muzzle velocity, their round shot was intended to create many deadly wooden splinters when hitting the structure of an enemy vessel, leading to the nickname "the smasher."

cleats: strips of wood, iron or other material fastened across something to give strength, hold in position or furnish a grip.

clipper: a very fast sailing ship of the nineteenth century that had multiple masts and square sails.

Colón: a seaport in Panama at the Atlantic end of the Panama Canal.

coyote: used for a man who has the sneaking and skulking characteristics of a coyote.

cutlass: a short, heavy, slightly curved sword with a single cutting edge, formerly used by sailors.

dick: a detective.

doffed chapeaus: removal of one's hat; following the rules of etiquette regarding the wearing of hats and when one should remove them.

dope: information, data or news.

fantail: a rounded overhanging part of a ship's stern (the rear part of the ship).

flatfoot: a police officer; cop; a patrolman walking a regular beat.

flophouse: a cheap, run-down hotel or rooming house.

forty-five or **.45 automatic:** a handgun chambered to fire a .45-caliber cartridge and that utilizes the recoil or part of the force of the explosive to eject the spent cartridge shell, introduce a new cartridge, cock the arm and fire it repeatedly.

gangway: a narrow, movable platform or ramp forming a bridge by which to board or leave a ship.

G-men: government men; agents of the Federal Bureau of Investigation.

greenhorn: an easterner unacquainted with cowboy ways.

Guantánamo: Guantánamo Bay Naval Base at the southeastern end of Cuba. It has been used by the United States Navy since 1898 and is the oldest overseas US Navy base.

Gulf of Chihli: the innermost gulf of the Yellow Sea on the coast of northeastern China. Its proximity to Beijing, the capital of China, makes it one of the busiest seaways in the world.

gunwale: the upper edge of the side of a boat. Originally a gunwale was a platform where guns were mounted, and was designed to accommodate the additional stresses imposed by the artillery being used.

Haiti: country in the Caribbean occupying the western part of the island of Hispaniola. The other half is occupied by the Dominican Republic.

half-seas over: almost drunk.

halyard: a rope used for raising and lowering a sail.

hawser: a thick rope or cable for mooring or towing a ship.

Horn, the: Cape Horn; the southern tip of South America. The passage around Cape Horn is one of the most hazardous shipping routes in the world, however, the use of this route was greatly reduced by the opening of the Panama Canal in 1914. It is commonly known to sailors simply as *the Horn*.

Huangpu: a long river in China flowing through Shanghai. It is a major navigational route, lined with wharves, warehouses and industrial plants, and provides access to Shanghai for oceangoing vessels.

inboard: within the hull or toward the center of a vessel.

Insular Line: US shipping line established in 1904.

jake: satisfactory; okay; fine.

Judge Advocate General or **JAG:** senior legal advisor to a branch of the military.

Judge Colt: nickname for the single-action (that is, cocked by hand for each shot), six-shot Army model revolver first produced in 1873 by Colt Firearms Company, the armory founded by Samuel Colt (1814–1862). The handgun of the Old West became the instrument of both lawmaker and lawbreaker during the last twenty-five years of the nineteenth century. It soon earned various names, such as "Peacemaker," "Equalizer," and "Judge Colt and his jury of six."

junks: seagoing ships with traditional Chinese designs and used primarily in Chinese waters. Junks have square sails, a high stern and usually a flat bottom.

keelhauled: a severe form of corporal punishment meted out to sailors at sea. The sailor was tied to a rope that looped beneath the vessel, thrown overboard on one side of the ship and dragged under the ship's keel to the other side. As the hull was often covered with barnacles and other marine growth, this could result in lacerations and other injuries.

letters of mark and reprisal: a license to a private citizen to seize property of another nation.

lit out: left in a hurry.

midshipman: a student naval officer educated principally at sea.

oakum: loose hemp or jute fiber, sometimes treated with tar or asphalt, used chiefly for caulking seams in wooden ships.

outs, been on the: been estranged from another person; been unfriendly or on bad terms with.

painter: a rope, usually at the bow, for fastening a boat to a ship, stake, etc.

paper suitcase: an inexpensive suitcase made of hard cardboard.

privateersman: an armed ship that is privately owned and manned, commissioned by a government to fight or harass enemy ships.

ratlines: small ropes fastened horizontally between the shrouds in the rigging of a sailing ship to form ladder rungs for the crew going aloft.

rowels: the small spiked revolving wheels on the ends of spurs, which are attached to the heels of a rider's boots and used to nudge a horse into going faster.

Scheherazade: the female narrator of *The Arabian Nights,* who during one thousand and one adventurous nights saved her life by entertaining her husband, the king, with stories.

scuttle: to sink a ship by making holes through the bottom.

shorthorn: a tenderfoot; a newcomer or a person not used to rough living and hardships.

slickers: swindlers; sly cheats.

slug: a bullet.

SS: steamship.

stanchion: an upright bar, post or frame forming a support or barrier.

stem to stern, from: from one end of the ship to the other or through the whole length.

superstructure: cabins and rooms above the deck of a ship.

Thames: a river of southern England flowing eastward to a wide estuary on the North Sea. Navigable for large ships as far as London, it is the principal commercial waterway of the country.

thirty-eight or **.38:** Police Positive .38; a .38-caliber revolver developed by the Colt Firearms Company in answer to a demand for a more powerful version of the .32-caliber Police Positive. First introduced in 1905, these guns were sold to many US police forces and European military units, as well as being made available to the general public.

thwart: a seat across a boat, especially one used by a rower.

twenty-five or **.25 automatic:** a small handgun chambered for the .25 ACP (Automatic Colt Pistol) cartridge designed by American firearms inventor John M. Browning (1855–1926).

USS: United States Steamship.

well deck: the space on the main deck of a ship lying at a lower level between the bridge and either a raised forward deck or a raised deck at the stern, which usually has cabins underneath.

West Indies rum: rum made by the West Indies Rum Distillery Limited. Established in 1893 by the Stades brothers, its primary purpose was to export rum to their homeland of Germany. Introducing the first still to the Caribbean, they were pioneers in scientific rum making.

wing collar: a shirt collar, used especially in men's formal clothing, in which the front edges are folded down in such a way as to resemble a pair of wings.

Yellow Sea: an arm of the Pacific Ocean between the Chinese mainland and the Korean Peninsula. It connects with the East China Sea to the south.

L. Ron Hubbard
in the Golden Age
of Pulp Fiction

*In writing an adventure story
a writer has to know that he is adventuring
for a lot of people who cannot.
The writer has to take them here and there
about the globe and show them
excitement and love and realism.
As long as that writer is living the part of an
adventurer when he is hammering
the keys, he is succeeding with his story.*

*Adventuring is a state of mind.
If you adventure through life, you have a
good chance to be a success on paper.*

*Adventure doesn't mean globe-trotting,
exactly, and it doesn't mean great deeds.
Adventuring is like art.
You have to live it to make it real.*

—*L. RON HUBBARD*

L. Ron Hubbard
and American
Pulp Fiction

B ORN March 13, 1911, L. Ron Hubbard lived a life at least as expansive as the stories with which he enthralled a hundred million readers through a fifty-year career.

Originally hailing from Tilden, Nebraska, he spent his formative years in a classically rugged Montana, replete with the cowpunchers, lawmen and desperadoes who would later people his Wild West adventures. And lest anyone imagine those adventures were drawn from vicarious experience, he was not only breaking broncs at a tender age, he was also among the few whites ever admitted into Blackfoot society as a bona fide blood brother. While if only to round out an otherwise rough and tumble youth, his mother was that rarity of her time—a thoroughly educated woman—who introduced her son to the classics of Occidental literature even before his seventh birthday.

But as any dedicated L. Ron Hubbard reader will attest, his world extended far beyond Montana. In point of fact, and as the son of a United States naval officer, by the age of eighteen he had traveled over a quarter of a million miles. Included therein were three Pacific crossings to a then still mysterious Asia, where he ran with the likes of Her British Majesty's agent-in-place

L. Ron Hubbard, left, at Congressional Airport, Washington, DC, 1931, with members of George Washington University flying club.

for North China, and the last in the line of Royal Magicians from the court of Kublai Khan. For the record, L. Ron Hubbard was also among the first Westerners to gain admittance to forbidden Tibetan monasteries below Manchuria, and his photographs of China's Great Wall long graced American geography texts.

Upon his return to the United States and a hasty completion of his interrupted high school education, the young Ron Hubbard entered George Washington University. There, as fans of his aerial adventures may have heard, he earned his wings as a pioneering barnstormer at the dawn of American aviation. He also earned a place in free-flight record books for the longest sustained flight above Chicago. Moreover, as a roving reporter for *Sportsman Pilot* (featuring his first professionally penned articles), he further helped inspire a generation of pilots who would take America to world airpower.

Immediately beyond his sophomore year, Ron embarked on the first of his famed ethnological expeditions, initially to then untrammeled Caribbean shores (descriptions of which would later fill a whole series of West Indies mystery-thrillers). That the Puerto Rican interior would also figure into the future of Ron Hubbard stories was likewise no accident. For in addition to cultural studies of the island, a 1932–33

LRH expedition is rightly remembered as conducting the first complete mineralogical survey of a Puerto Rico under United States jurisdiction.

There was many another adventure along this vein: As a lifetime member of the famed Explorers Club, L. Ron Hubbard charted North Pacific waters with the first shipboard radio direction finder, and so pioneered a long-range navigation system universally employed until the late twentieth century. While not to put too fine an edge on it, he also held a rare Master Mariner's license to pilot any vessel, of any tonnage in any ocean.

Yet lest we stray too far afield, there is an LRH note at this juncture in his saga, and it reads in part:

"I started out writing for the pulps, writing the best I knew, writing for every mag on the stands, slanting as well as I could."

Capt. L. Ron Hubbard in Ketchikan, Alaska, 1940, on his Alaskan Radio Experimental Expedition, the first of three voyages conducted under the Explorers Club flag.

To which one might add: His earliest submissions date from the summer of 1934, and included tales drawn from true-to-life Asian adventures, with characters roughly modeled on British/American intelligence operatives he had known in Shanghai. His early Westerns were similarly peppered with details drawn from personal experience. Although therein lay a first hard lesson from the often cruel world of the pulps. His first Westerns were soundly rejected as lacking the authenticity of a Max Brand yarn (a particularly frustrating comment given L. Ron Hubbard's Westerns came straight from his Montana homeland, while Max Brand was a mediocre New York poet named Frederick Schiller Faust, who turned out implausible six-shooter tales from the terrace of an Italian villa).

Nevertheless, and needless to say, L. Ron Hubbard persevered and soon earned a reputation as among the most publishable names in pulp fiction, with a ninety percent placement rate of first-draft manuscripts. He was also among the most prolific, averaging between seventy and a hundred thousand words a month. Hence the rumors that L. Ron Hubbard had redesigned a typewriter for faster keyboard action and pounded out manuscripts on a continuous roll of butcher paper to save the precious seconds it took to insert a single sheet of paper into manual typewriters of the day.

That all L. Ron Hubbard stories did not run beneath said byline is yet another aspect of pulp fiction lore. That is, as publishers periodically rejected manuscripts from top-drawer authors if only to avoid paying top dollar, L. Ron Hubbard and company just as frequently replied with submissions under various pseudonyms. In Ron's case, the

---

A MAN OF MANY NAMES

Between 1934 and 1950, L. Ron Hubbard authored more than fifteen million words of fiction in more than two hundred classic publications. To supply his fans and editors with stories across an array of genres and pulp titles, he adopted fifteen pseudonyms in addition to his already renowned L. Ron Hubbard byline.

Winchester Remington Colt
Lt. Jonathan Daly
Capt. Charles Gordon
Capt. L. Ron Hubbard
Bernard Hubbel
Michael Keith
Rene Lafayette
Legionnaire 148
Legionnaire 14830
Ken Martin
Scott Morgan
Lt. Scott Morgan
Kurt von Rachen
Barry Randolph
Capt. Humbert Reynolds

list included: Rene Lafayette, Captain Charles Gordon, Lt. Scott Morgan and the notorious Kurt von Rachen—supposedly on the lam for a murder rap, while hammering out two-fisted prose in Argentina. The point: While L. Ron Hubbard as Ken Martin spun stories of Southeast Asian intrigue, LRH as Barry Randolph authored tales of romance on the Western range—which, stretching between a dozen genres is how he came to stand among the two hundred elite authors providing close to a million tales through the glory days of American Pulp Fiction.

L. Ron Hubbard, circa 1930, at the outset of a literary career that would finally span half a century.

In evidence of exactly that, by 1936 L. Ron Hubbard was literally leading pulp fiction's elite as president of New York's American Fiction Guild. Members included a veritable pulp hall of fame: Lester "Doc Savage" Dent, Walter "The Shadow" Gibson, and the legendary Dashiell Hammett—to cite but a few.

Also in evidence of just where L. Ron Hubbard stood within his first two years on the American pulp circuit: By the spring of 1937, he was ensconced in Hollywood, adopting a Caribbean thriller for Columbia Pictures, remembered today as *The Secret of Treasure Island*. Comprising fifteen thirty-minute episodes, the L. Ron Hubbard screenplay led to the most profitable matinée serial in Hollywood history. In accord with Hollywood culture, he was thereafter continually called upon

The 1937 Secret of Treasure Island, *a fifteen-episode serial adapted for the screen by L. Ron Hubbard from his novel,* Murder at Pirate Castle.

to rewrite/doctor scripts—most famously for long-time friend and fellow adventurer Clark Gable.

In the interim—and herein lies another distinctive chapter of the L. Ron Hubbard story—he continually worked to open Pulp Kingdom gates to up-and-coming authors. Or, for that matter, anyone who wished to write. It was a fairly unconventional stance, as markets were already thin and competition razor sharp. But the fact remains, it was an L. Ron Hubbard hallmark that he vehemently lobbied on behalf of young authors—regularly supplying instructional articles to trade journals, guest-lecturing to short story classes at George Washington University and Harvard, and even founding his own creative writing competition. It was established in 1940, dubbed the Golden Pen, and guaranteed winners both New York representation and publication in *Argosy*.

But it was John W. Campbell Jr.'s *Astounding Science Fiction* that finally proved the most memorable LRH vehicle. While every fan of L. Ron Hubbard's galactic epics undoubtedly knows the story, it nonetheless bears repeating: By late 1938, the pulp publishing magnate of Street & Smith was determined to revamp *Astounding Science Fiction* for broader readership. In particular, senior editorial director F. Orlin Tremaine called for stories with a stronger *human element*. When acting editor John W. Campbell balked, preferring his spaceship-driven tales, Tremaine enlisted Hubbard. Hubbard, in turn, replied with the genre's first truly *character-driven* works, wherein heroes are pitted not against bug-eyed monsters but the mystery and majesty of deep space itself—and thus was launched the Golden Age of Science Fiction.

The names alone are enough to quicken the pulse of any science fiction aficionado, including LRH friend and protégé, Robert Heinlein, Isaac Asimov, A. E. van Vogt and Ray Bradbury. Moreover, when coupled with LRH stories of fantasy, we further come to what's rightly been described as the

foundation of every modern tale of horror: L. Ron Hubbard's immortal *Fear*. It was rightly proclaimed by Stephen King as one of the very few works to genuinely warrant that overworked term "classic"—as in: *"This is a classic tale of creeping, surreal menace and horror. . . . This is one of the really, really good ones."*

L. Ron Hubbard, 1948, among fellow science fiction luminaries at the World Science Fiction Convention in Toronto.

To accommodate the greater body of L. Ron Hubbard fantasies, Street & Smith inaugurated *Unknown*—a classic pulp if there ever was one, and wherein readers were soon thrilling to the likes of *Typewriter in the Sky* and *Slaves of Sleep* of which Frederik Pohl would declare: *"There are bits and pieces from Ron's work that became part of the language in ways that very few other writers managed."*

And, indeed, at J. W. Campbell Jr.'s insistence, Ron was regularly drawing on themes from the Arabian Nights and so introducing readers to a world of genies, jinn, Aladdin and Sinbad—all of which, of course, continue to float through cultural mythology to this day.

At least as influential in terms of post-apocalypse stories was L. Ron Hubbard's 1940 *Final Blackout*. Generally acclaimed as the finest anti-war novel of the decade and among the ten best works of the genre ever authored—here, too, was a tale that would live on in ways few other writers imagined.

Hence, the later Robert Heinlein verdict: "Final Blackout *is as perfect a piece of science fiction as has ever been written.*"

Like many another who both lived and wrote American pulp adventure, the war proved a tragic end to Ron's sojourn in the pulps. He served with distinction in four theaters and was highly decorated for commanding corvettes in the North Pacific. He was also grievously wounded in combat, lost many a close friend and colleague and thus resolved to say farewell to pulp fiction and devote himself to what it had supported these many years—namely, his serious research.

Portland, Oregon, 1943; L. Ron Hubbard, captain of the US Navy subchaser PC 815.

But in no way was the LRH literary saga at an end, for as he wrote some thirty years later, in 1980:

"Recently there came a period when I had little to do. This was novel in a life so crammed with busy years, and I decided to amuse myself by writing a novel that was pure *science fiction."*

That work was *Battlefield Earth: A Saga of the Year 3000*. It was an immediate *New York Times* bestseller and, in fact, the first international science fiction blockbuster in decades. It was not, however, L. Ron Hubbard's magnum opus, as that distinction is generally reserved for his next and final work: The 1.2 million word *Mission Earth*.

> **Final Blackout**
> *is as perfect a piece of science fiction as has ever been written.*
>
> —Robert Heinlein

How he managed those 1.2 million words in just over twelve months is yet another piece of the L. Ron Hubbard legend. But the fact remains, he did indeed author a ten-volume *dekalogy* that lives in publishing history for the fact that each and every volume of the series was also a *New York Times* bestseller.

Moreover, as subsequent generations discovered L. Ron Hubbard through republished works and novelizations of his screenplays, the mere fact of his name on a cover signaled an international bestseller. . . . Until, to date, sales of his works exceed hundreds of millions, and he otherwise remains among the most enduring and widely read authors in literary history. Although as a final word on the tales of L. Ron Hubbard, perhaps it's enough to simply reiterate what editors told readers in the glory days of American Pulp Fiction:

He writes the way he does, brothers, because he's been there, seen it and done it!

THE STORIES FROM THE GOLDEN AGE

Your ticket to adventure starts here with the Stories from
the Golden Age collection by master storyteller L. Ron Hubbard.
These gripping tales are set in a kaleidoscope of exotic locales and brim
with fascinating characters, including some of the
most vile villains, dangerous dames and brazen heroes
you'll ever get to meet.

The entire collection of over one hundred and fifty stories is being
released in a series of eighty books and audiobooks.
For an up-to-date listing of available titles,
go to www.goldenagestories.com.

AIR ADVENTURE

FAR-FLUNG ADVENTURE

SEA ADVENTURE

TALES FROM THE ORIENT

MYSTERY

111

FANTASY

SCIENCE FICTION

WESTERN

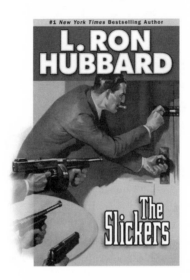

JOIN THE PULP REVIVAL
America in the 1930s and 40s

Pulp fiction was in its heyday and 30 million readers were regularly riveted by the larger-than-life tales of master storyteller L. Ron Hubbard. For this was pulp fiction's golden age, when the writing was raw and every page packed a walloping punch.

That magic can now be yours. An evocative world of nefarious villains, exotic intrigues, courageous heroes and heroines—a world that today's cinema has barely tapped for tales of adventure and swashbucklers.

Enroll today in the Stories from the Golden Age Club and begin receiving your monthly feature edition selected from more than 150 stories in the collection.

You may choose to enjoy them as either a paperback or audiobook for the special membership price of $9.95 each month along with FREE shipping and handling.